BLESSED BY MALAKAI

TO MARRY A MADDEN SERIES

SHERELLE GREEN

Editor: There for You Editing

Cover Design: Sherelle Green

Manufactured and Printed in the United States of America

To my readers who fiercely love the Madden men.
This series is for you!

DEAR READER

The outpouring of love and support for Micah Madden (hero in Red Velvet Kisses) and Malik Madden (hero in Beautiful Surrender) from my Elite Events series was amazing!

After a long wait, I'm excited to share Malakai Madden's story and introduce you to this new spin-off series, To Marry A Madden!

I had so much fun writing Malakai's story, so I hope you enjoy this one :).

#BLESSEDBYMALAKAI

Every man has his weakness. For prominent painter and sculptor Malakai Madden, that weakness has always been women. Now, he's finally ready to settle down and shower one woman with his love. There's just one major problem. Overnight, he's gained thousands of Twitter followers after his obsessive ex decides to leak some private information. To make matters worse, a well-known media source retweets them! Suddenly, every woman wants a piece of Malakai. And when the #BlessedByMalakai hashtag starts trending, he's dodging women left and right, and blocking his crotch like he's secret service securing the president. If he's ever going to get his life back and find his future wife, he needs to solve this problem and he needs to solve it fast!

Image consultant Avery Nightingale can't believe she's landed a meeting with a huge potential client. She knows all about the #BlessedByMalakai hashtag and she's ready to pitch her ideas. However, when she meets the man behind the Twitter legend, she's rendered speechless and Mr. Make You Moan is not impressed. He agrees to hire her on one condition. Avery must promise not to feed into the social media craze as others have failed to accomplish before her. She agrees. After all, it's just one rule, right?

ONE

Malakai

I'm no gentleman. Never have been. Granted, if you asked the people who know me best, they would say that I hold open doors for women, I respect my elders, I donate to several charities, and I'm always there for the people I love. But make no mistake. I'm no gentleman. At least not in the bedroom.

I'd never apologize for my desire to fulfill a woman's needs and fantasies by making every intimate moment we share better than the last. And until today, I'd never questioned my sexual escapades. Up until today, I'd never thought twice about leaving a woman so satisfied, she couldn't help but boast about me to her friends. Up until today, I would have sworn that there was nothing wrong with a woman feeling like a night with me meant unlimited orgasms *guaranteed*.

Too bad that today, the unthinkable happened. Today,

with each passing minute, I was regretting the fact that I was so good at what I do. I loved women. I appreciated women. But in this moment, I'd do anything to change my past actions and re-evaluate the steps I took that landed me in my current predicament.

Run faster, I thought to myself, taking longer strides and trying my best to block out all of the voices yelling behind me.

"Malakai Madden, you're a sex god!"

"Malakai Madden, I want to have your babies."

"Oh my God, Malakai, I want to be blessed by you."

The last comment made me turn around and face the mob of women who were currently chasing after me on one of the busiest streets in downtown Chicago.

"Ladies, this is a bit much. Don't you think?" I yelled behind me. In the wave of "no's" that echoed through the crowd, I heard a voice I recognized. The voice of the woman who started this crazy mess in the first place.

"Malakai, choose me," Roxanne yelled over the women. "Marry me. Love me. You know we're perfect together."

I shook my head as I picked up speed and prayed that Bare Sophistication, the lingerie boutique my cousin's owned, was open considering it was so early in the morning. Out of the corner of my eye, I caught two police officers on a side street directing morning traffic.

"I'm so glad to see you fellas," I called, approaching the police officers. "A crazy mob of women has been chasing me for several blocks. Is there anything you can do to make them stop?"

"I know you," one of the police officers said. "You're that guy who is all over the internet right now."

"That's right," the other cop interjected. "They were talking about you on the news."

"Right." I glanced over my shoulder at the women growing nearer. Not only was I out of breath, but the tailored, one-of-a-kind suit that I was wearing for an important meeting I had was constricting, which meant I couldn't run as fast as I needed to run.

"Here's the thing," I said, slightly breathless. "Because of that internet mishap, I had random women knocking on the door of my hotel room all night. At first, I was pissed that the hotel had given out my room number, until I realized the women knocking all worked for the hotel. Then, my iPhone was constantly ringing off the hook to the point that I cut the damn thing off even though I need my phone to do business. I thought the hype would die down by the morning, but the moment I stepped into the lobby of my hotel, I was approached by the women you see running toward us right now and they have been chasing me ever since."

The police officers laughed, and the sound made me grind my teeth together. "Doesn't seem like a bad problem to have to me. Not sure what you want us to do."

My gaze bounced from one to the other. "Isn't it disturbing the peace by having a group of people running through intersections and cutting off the traffic flow?"

The skinny officer shrugged.

"What about giving them jaywalking tickets?"

"Then we'd have to give you one, too, according to what you've told us," the officer replied.

"Fine by me," I stated as calmly as possible. "Anything to end this morning from hell."

A squeal from a separate group of women to my left caught all our attention. "Not again," I whispered, noticing that look of recognition on a couple of the women's faces who'd just walked out of their office building.

The heftier police officer peered over his shoulder. "On second thought, we don't see anything wrong. It looks to me as if this is one of the most exciting things to happen downtown in a while."

What the hell? "What about my well-being? I could be running for miles before they stop."

Instead of responding, each of the officers laughed. Concluding that neither of them were willing to help me, I took off running just as one officer asked if we could take a selfie together.

"I really worry about America right now," I huffed as I took a shortcut through an alley, almost running over a man taking out his garbage.

"Hey, watch yourself," the older gentleman yelled.

"Sorry," I called back. I glanced over my shoulder in time to see the herd of women knock him over, a few tumbling to the ground as they did so. A part of me thought this collision would make them stop, yet, the few who had fallen simply brushed off their knees, jumped right back up, and continued after me.

"This can't be real life." When I reached another busy road, I was slightly disoriented. It took a minute to realize that I'd walked into an area that was in the process of being set up for a food and wine festival occurring in a few days.

Glancing down at my cap toe Stacy Adams shoes, I cursed at the unfortunate events that had transpired in thirty-six hours. Now that I'd taken a detour, my cousins' lingerie boutique wasn't close anymore, but as luck would have it, I noticed that my brother's security firm was only a couple blocks away.

I need a distraction, I thought as I dodged in between two large semi-trucks that were being unloaded.

"Hey, man," I said to this young cat who couldn't have been more than twenty or twenty-one years old.

His eyes widened as if he recognized me, but to his credit, he didn't mention how. "Hello, sir."

"Hey." I pulled out a hundred-dollar bill. "I know you're working, but is there any way you could do me a solid and let me hide in this truck until the herd of women following me passes by?"

He looked skeptical at first, but he agreed. The feeling of relief that overwhelmed me was the best I'd felt all morning.

"What's your name?" I asked.

"Will," he replied.

I nodded in thanks. "Thank you, Will."

"No problem. I'll give you a holla when the coast is clear."

I almost wanted to hug him, but I knew it was just my adrenaline talking. Wasting no time, I passed him the hundred and climbed into the truck, hiding behind items that were waiting to be unloaded.

I loosened my tie, my heart beating out of my chest as I heard the voices of the women grow nearer. *This is a damn shame.* Who would have ever thought they'd see the day when Malakai Madden was hiding from a group of women?

I should have stayed my ass in New York. Business had brought me to Chicago, and since I had family in the area, it seemed like a great idea to stay for a little while and visit my siblings and cousins. Had I known that shit would hit the fan and I'd be dodging women left and right, I would have skipped this project and found myself a nice secluded bungalow in the Caribbean.

"Have you seen Malakai?"

I ducked deeper into the semi as I heard a woman ask Will where I was.

"Nah, I didn't see him," Will lied.

"Are you sure?" another woman asked. "He had to have come right past you."

"Maybe he's in the truck," a third woman chimed in.

Shit. In the midst of all the commotion, it dawned on me that I hadn't created an exit strategy when I'd gotten into this truck. There was only one way in and one way out, so if the women decided to search it, I couldn't escape.

"On second thought," Will began, "I think I saw him run that way."

I had no idea which way Will pointed, but I couldn't care less if it got them off my back.

"Let's go, ladies," one of them yelled. Soon, I heard the noise grow fainter as they left the semi.

I still felt as though I was on the brink of a heart attack as I waited for any indication that it was okay to leave. After a couple minutes, I assumed that Will had forgotten to give me the okay, so I proceeded to exit the truck.

It only took me a few seconds to assess the situation and realize that Will had still been looking out for me and my ass should have stayed in the back of the semi.

"There he is," a reporter yelled, turning from Will to me as I hopped out of the truck. "There's Malakai Madden."

The next thirty seconds seemed to happen in slow motion as I watched a group of reporters stumble over one another to get close to me.

"Mr. Madden, how does it feel to be the latest internet sensation?"

"Malakai, do you consider yourself a player or a one-woman man?"

"Malakai, you're a prominent artist and your clientele

include a lot of celebrities and high-profile politicians. But how do you think the release of this news will affect the churches and schools you do business with?"

I stood speechless as cameras flashed in my face and microphones were thrust in front of me. My mind could barely comprehend the questions being asked. I couldn't move as I thought about how much my life had been flipped upside down in thirty-six hours.

The lump in my throat made it hard for me to swallow as I contemplated the implications the internet madness would have on the personal goals I'd recently set for myself. Even worse, I couldn't begin to wrap my head around how this would affect my career.

I glanced over at Will who shrugged his shoulders in pity. I'd barely spoken with the dude, but today, he'd seen me at my worse. *This can't be happening.* I refused to think my life could change so much from a few tweets, but as I looked out over the crowd gathering to see what all of the fuss was about, I knew that was exactly what had happened.

Most men would love to have the media interested in interviewing them for such a spicy story. Most men would welcome a herd of women flocking behind him every second of the day. Most men would enjoy hearing women yell things that were better suited for bedroom banter, rather than in public.

"Malakai Madden, do you have anything to say?"

Too bad I wasn't most men.

TWO

Malakai

36 Hours Prior ...

"FELLAS, it's official. This year, I'm finally going to settle down and shower one woman with my love."

The poker table grew quiet the moment the words left my lips. Although I lived in New York, I was often in Chicago on business. My two older brothers, Malik and Micah, had both made the city their home after falling in love with two of the four co-founders and owners of Elite Events Incorporated.

The three of us used to all be on the same page, but after they'd both gotten married, our conversations changed from discussing getting ass and the latest news in sports to the best daycares in the area and the quickest way to organize your garage.

Okay, maybe I was exaggerating slightly, but it was true that they weren't the same men they were years ago. They were even better. Tonight, the game was being held at our friend Shawn's place. Shawn was also married to one of the Elite Events co-founders and Daman—although he hadn't arrived yet—rounded off as the fourth Elite Events husband.

"Dude, quit playin'," my brother Micah said, shaking his head.

I shrugged. "I'm not. I've been giving this a lot of thought and I really think it's time for me to settle down."

Seemingly realizing the seriousness in my tone, Malik and Shawn placed their cards face down on the table.

I placed my cards down as well. "I'm serious, fellas. I'm thirty-four and I'm not getting any younger. It's time for me to find *the one*."

"One what?" Malik asked. "Because last time Mom mentioned you finding a wife, you told her the day you marry will be the day hell freezes over."

"Yeah, well, in case y'all haven't been paying attention to politics lately, number forty-five being chosen to run our country proves that hell has frozen over."

Malik nodded his head. "Point taken."

We all grew quiet at the table.

"So you're serious?" Shawn asked, breaking the silence. "You're ready to stop playing the field?" Although I'd met Shawn through my brothers, we'd grown close over the years. It was safe to say that he knew me almost as well as they did.

"I'm serious," I replied. "I plan to be married within the next year." It was no secret that although I liked to call myself carefree, the truth was, I lived life more calculated than most. It wasn't unusual for me to have a timeline for when I needed to accomplish certain goals I'd set for myself.

"I'll get us a few more beers while y'all talk some sense into him," Shawn said, standing from his seat and directing his attention to Malik and Micah. "Although I understand him wanting to settle down, buddy ass is trippin' if he thinks he can rush falling in love based off his timeline."

Malik stroked his hand down his face. "Malakai, you do know what settling down means, right?"

"Man, yeah. I know what it means. And I'm serious. I'm tired of playing the field. It's time for me to follow in my big brothers' footsteps and find me a wife."

Micah snorted. "I'm not buying it. Why now?"

Just as I was going to answer, I received a FaceTime call. "Shit, it's Roxanne."

"Your crazy ex who stood outside your place in New York and serenaded you all night?" Shawn asked, returning with the beers.

"The one and only," I replied, all humor gone from my voice. "Calling Roxanne an ex is putting it nicely."

"You damn right." Micah shook his head. "Roxanne is more like a crazy stalker who Malakai made the mistake of sleeping with. Repeatedly."

"I didn't know she would turn out to be crazy," I said, looking from my brothers to Shawn.

"Yes, you did." Malik laughed before glancing at Shawn. "This is the woman we told you about who Malakai met a couple years ago at a lounge here in Chicago right after he created that sculpture for rap artist and actor, Common. We were out celebrating and she popped up in the VIP section claiming to be a fan. Micah and I could tell she was one of the stalker fans, but Malaki didn't listen. Not only did he hook up with her that night, but she followed him to Chicago. And now, she pops up all the time at different locations he's at and they have an on-again-off-again relationship."

I raised one of my hands in defense as my phone finally stopped ringing. "I wouldn't say relationship."

"Well, a fuckship then," Micah added. "Or friends with benefits. Heavy on the benefits. Malik was trying to save face for you, but I give it to you straight."

Malakai frowned. "No friends. Just benefits."

Shawn shook his head. "Regardless, why the hell did you continue to mess with her if she had all the signs of a stalker?"

I looked at my brothers, the three of us sharing a smirk as we thought about the reason I put up with Roxanne's craziness. "That ass though," we all said in unison before busting out into laughter.

"I see." Shawn laughed along with us. "Men will do anything for the booty."

We all sighed, each caught in our own thoughts. The problem with my thoughts were that I wasn't thinking about my wife like I knew my brothers and Shawn were. I didn't really have a face to go along with my thoughts, so all I could do was imagine what my future wife might look like.

The sound of another FaceTime call coming through my phone broke the moment. I ground my teeth together when I recognized the same number that had called me before. "It's Roxanne again."

"If you don't answer, she's going to keep calling," Micah stated.

Concluding he was right, I reluctantly answered. "Hey, Roxanne."

"Lovebug," she said in a baby voice. "You've been avoiding my calls."

I didn't even have to look at the guys to know they were silently laughing to themselves. "I've been busy, Roxanne.

And I thought I asked you to stop calling me. What we had is over."

"I don't want it to be over," she pleaded. "And I'm in Chicago and want to see you."

I mentally slapped my forehead although what I really wanted to do was throw my damn phone across the room. "Roxanne, I've told you time and time again to stop following me to every city I go to. I'll press charges if I need to."

"Don't be like that, snickerdoodle. You know that you and I are meant to be together. Don't fight it."

Meant to be together? Hell nah. "I'm sure there is a man out there for you, but that man isn't me."

"Only if that man doesn't mind being followed everywhere he goes," Malik whispered.

"And sleeping with one eye open," Micah added.

I ignored my brothers before continuing. "Roxanne, I'm determined to find the right woman for me, which means, whatever you think we have going on is over. I'm ready to love one woman and one woman only. A woman who accepts me for who I am and isn't afraid to tell the world why she loves me. In shorter terms, I'm looking for my wife and as harsh as it sounds, that woman isn't you."

Shawn shook her head. "Bruh, you're telling her too much."

"It is me," Roxanne whined. "Malakai, if you're looking for a wife, you've already found her. And I'm not afraid to tell the world how much I love you."

This time, I rubbed my forehead, not caring that she could see the stress written across my face through the Face-Time call. "Roxanne, that's not necessary. We're over and we've been over for a while. It's time for you to move on."

Although I'd hoped she finally got the message loud and

clear, the sneaky gleam in her eyes proved that she was far from understanding.

"Well, we'll just see about that, my chocolate Adonis. Ta ta for now." When she blew me a kiss, it took all of my energy not to reach into the air, pretend to grab it, and smash it in my hand.

It hadn't even been a full two seconds after Roxanne disconnected the call before the men began laughing.

"She's a piece of work," Shawn said. "If she truly is crazy like you say, you definitely told her too much information."

"For the most part, she's harmless." I picked my cards back up. "Anyway, can we get back to the game and stop talking about me?"

"Whatever you say, chocolate Adonis," Micah said with a wink.

I tossed a potato chip at him. "Man, enough with that. Let's play."

The men nodded, and soon, it was back to business as usual. Knowing my brothers, I figured they would eventually want to talk about the fact that I wanted to get married within the next year, but at least for tonight we were done.

An hour later, Daman finally arrived. He quickly greeted Shawn before coming over to the poker table like a man on a mission. "Bruh, what the hell did you do to crazy Roxanne?"

Daman had been there the night we had met Roxanne, so I wasn't surprised he still remembered who she was. Like Shawn, I'd grown closer to Daman as well, and I often teased the four of them about being the husbands of Elite Events since their wives were the queens of event planning.

"I didn't do anything," I replied, shrugging my shoulders. "Why do you ask?"

Daman scrolled through his phone. "Because an hour ago, Roxanne started posting a bunch of mess on Twitter and tagged you in her tweets. Now, the hashtag she started is blowing up."

I grabbed Daman's phone hoping he was just exaggerating. "Get the fuck out of here. Is she seriously tweeting about the times we've had sex?"

"Yep," Daman said. "And now, Roxanne isn't the only one."

As I scrolled through Daman's Twitter account, my mouth literally dried up. "Oh shit, she started the #BlessedByMalakai hashtag an hour ago and it's already trending."

"Apparently, she's doing this to try and win your love," Shawn said, glancing through his own phone. "She says as much in her first tweets."

I'd just landed on the same tweets Shawn mentioned, noticing she had tweeted at least ten more times.

@MalakaiMadden is looking for love
and he wants a wife who isn't afraid to
share her feelings with the world.
#BlessedByMalakai

Ladies, in case you didn't know
@MalakaiMadden is a #SexGod.
No dick is as good as his dick.
His penis should be gold plated.
#GoldPlatedPenis #BlessedByMalakai

> I was #BlessedByMalakai a couple years
> ago and I've been addicted to
> the D ever since. #FutureMrsMadden #IDoItForTheD

"IT SEEMS like other women are following her lead," Daman remarked.

"Some of the other women are women I've slept with," I said, my mouth hanging slightly open. "And they are detailing the time or times we've slept together to try and win my love." I couldn't believe what I was reading, but even closing my eyes and reopening them didn't make it go away.

> I was #BlessedByMalakai a few years ago
> when I was at a work convention. He took
> me on the balcony. Left me craving more.
> #unbelieveableexperience

> It was a warm June morning on the
> beach when I was #BlessedByMalakai.
> The sun was setting when I orgasmed.
> I still smile when the sun sets.

> Even though I'm married, my vagina still
> craves @MalakaiMadden. Glad I was able
> to be #BlessedByMalakai.

#BestSexEver #SorryHubby

I've never been #BlessedByMalakai, but I've seen him around New York before and would love the chance to see his dick in person. Or win his love. Whichever happens first.

Fuck love. I heard @MalakaiMadden has a big dick and I'm too busy to date. In need of a #onenightstand. Ready to be #BlessedByMalakai.

"OH THIS IS BAD." I sunk lower into my chair, unable to believe how many women had tweeted. "I never even said there was a contest to win my love. As a matter of fact, I haven't tweeted anything. Don't folks usually wait until they receive some sort of confirmation from the person in question?"

"Not on the internet," Shawn said. "Besides, World-StarHipHop and other popular media outlets are already retweeting Roxanne's tweets and others. It looks like folks are wondering if you'll settle down with an ex or someone new."

"I'm not famous, so I don't even understand why people are curious enough to entertain these tweets."

"You're famous enough, little brother." Malik reached for Daman's phone since he refused to get a Twitter account. Malik wasn't much for social media. "You've created sculptures and art pieces for a lot of famous people. And weren't you the one bragging last holiday about finally hitting that milestone of twitter followers?"

"Well yeah, but most of those followers follow me for my artwork or fashion. Not some lame ass tweets about my bedroom activity."

"Doesn't matter," Micah said. "The internet has no chill. People eat this shit up. Plus, with all of the reality television shows out now, it doesn't take much to become famous or trend whether you want the publicity or not."

I ran my hand over my trimmed beard the way I often did when I was nervous.

"And didn't you just get offered a chance to create an artistic mural for one of the state senators?" Malik asked.

"Crap, I forgot all about that," I muttered, my headache growing with each passing second. "I have to call my agent and make sure this doesn't jeopardize the deal. Although, I'm sure this will die down by tomorrow and the internet will find someone else to talk about."

"Ah, nah. I'm not so sure about that," Malik said, closing his eyes and thrusting the phone back at me. "Take the phone back."

"Why?" Micah asked, intercepting the phone and then following suit and closing his eyes as well. "Never mind. Here, Malakai."

I barely registered my fingers shaking as I glanced at the screen of the phone to see what had both of my brothers closing their eyes.

"Oh no." I wasn't the type of person who panicked easily, so I didn't even recognize the alarmed sound of my voice when I looked at the photo that Roxanne had just leaked.

Unlike before, I didn't close my eyes to try and make the photo go away. Closing my eyes wouldn't help. Saying a prayer wouldn't help. Deleting my Twitter account wouldn't help.

No matter what solution I thought of in my mind, nothing would change the fact that Roxanne had posted a picture of my dick that already had over five-hundred retweets and it hadn't even been a full minute.

"Is that really you?" Malik questioned since my head was cut off in the pic. *Thank God for that, I guess.*

"Yeah, it's me."

"Bruh, why would you send Roxanne's crazy ass a picture of your junk?" Micah was still rubbing his eyes after seeing the photo.

"I didn't," I said a lot calmer than I felt. "I can tell from the angle of the pic that I was sleep at the time."

"I thought you never slept over a woman's house or had them sleep over yours," Malik said.

"I don't." I looked closely at the bed sheets and night-stand, immediately recognizing where this had to have been taken. "When I had made the decision to stop messing with Roxanne a year ago, it was after she'd popped up on me in Miami. She asked me if we could get one more night together and I obliged. Per my usual, I asked her to leave after our good-bye fuck and she did so with no argument. The next morning, I woke up and found her in my bed. Apparently, she had stolen the key to my hotel room and let herself in after I'd fallen asleep."

"That's messed up." Shawn shook his head. "It's even more twisted that Roxanne would think she could be your wife after pulling a stunt like this. Why would she even think telling other women about sex with you would make you want to marry her more?"

"Why would she think you're even ready to get married?" Daman inquired, finally taking a seat at the only empty chair at the table.

All of the men looked to me for a response, yet, all I could do was stare back at the photo as five-hundred retweets turned to one thousand retweets. Which quickly turned to fifteen-hundred retweets. I reported the photo and messaged my agent, but I knew the internet never forgot once something like this was leaked.

The only thing that was true in all of this Twitter mess was the fact that I was blessed, or rather, well-endowed. Well, I guess some of the sexual recounts from my exes were true, too. But I liked my privacy and having this picture circulating on the internet was as far from private as it could get.

"How about I get us something to drink that's stronger than beers," Shawn suggested before heading to the kitchen. As my brothers went on to explain to Daman my desire to get married and how I'd ended up in my current predicament, all I could do was hope that tomorrow morning I would wake up and this would all be some terrible nightmare. I'd been eager to tell my brothers and friends that I was finally ready to settle down. Now, I wish I'd kept my damn mouth shut.

THREE

One year later ...

Avery

"COULD THIS DAY GET ANY WORSE," I huffed aloud as I wiped the spilled coffee from my yellow pencil skirt. The more I rubbed the damp spot, the worse it looked. *At least it got on my skirt and not my white blouse.* I'd been holding my piping hot cup of coffee for the past eight blocks, so it was a miracle I hadn't spilled it on myself as I walked.

Pushing my black rimmed glasses farther up on my nose, I took a few more steps until I reached a nearby café that was entirely too crowded and searched for a space on the wall that I could lean against. It was a nice and warm June day, but besides the weather, nothing was going right this morning. At this point, I didn't know why I expected anything less.

Frustrated, I closed my eyes and counted to ten to try and calm my frayed nerves. Ever since I'd made the leap six months ago to quit my full-time assistant job, move to New York City, and start my own PR agency, I'd run into more than a few obstacles.

First, I really wished someone would have told me that the apartments in New York were about the size of a storage locker. Second, New Yorkers walk fast. And I'm not talking about the brisk speed walk type of fast. I'm talking about the run-as-if-your-life-depends-on-it kind of fast. I walked holes into two pairs of good shoes my first month here.

Lastly, although I'd researched the cost of living, I hadn't thought that a simple chai-tea latte would cost five dollars more than it did in my Tennessee hometown. Although the creamy liquid slid down my throat in a way any previous latte never had, I knew a rip off when I saw one.

"Lady, watch the fuck where you're leaning!"

I opened my eyes and glanced up at the business suit who was holding his coffee in one hand and phone in another. I mouthed a simple *sorry* as I straightened my posture and adjusted my clothes, ready to tackle the New York streets again.

"Okay, Avery. You got this," I whispered to myself as I glanced at the tall skyscraper that was only a couple blocks away. After botching two client meetings this week, I really needed a break.

Some may call it being naïve, but in my mind, I thought within my first month of being in New York, I would land a huge client. Then, by six months, my name would already be floating around as one of the top young PR agents in the city. I had visions of me walking into a beautiful office with floor to ceiling windows while my assistant handed me a cup of coffee the moment I walked through the door.

"Keep on dreaming, girl." I slipped on my sunglasses and braved the streets again. Dreaming was good for the soul, however, the small table that folded down from the wall in my tiny apartment was hardly the beautiful office I'd imagined. And Sasha, my grey cat that had been with me for the past three years, hardly constituted as an assistant. On good days, I'd be lucky to even get her to move from her perch on my windowsill.

As I neared the tall, black building, my heart rate suddenly quickened. It was only this morning on the subway that I'd overheard a woman on the phone discussing how infamous creative artist Malakai Madden had fired yet another PR rep and was auditioning today to fill the vacancy.

On a whim, I'd decided that I needed to somehow get a chance to pitch to him that I was the best woman for the job, even if I didn't have an interview slot. My mom always said that it wasn't the early bird that got the worm. It was the most clever bird who ultimately won. So today, I planned on being the keenest bird in New York.

To some, what I was doing would be considered a smart move. To others, it would be a foolish one. I wasn't sure exactly which side of the coin I thought was more accurate, but regardless, I was going through with my plan.

"Excuse me." I wove around a few people who were standing outside of the office building. The lobby was buzzing with employees eager to kick off their lunch hour and take a break from work. Unfortunately, that also meant that security was on high alert as people swiped their badges to get in and out of the section leading to the elevators.

Shoot. Of course there's security, Avery. I mentally slapped myself on the forehead for not fully thinking this plan through. I'd been in enough of these buildings to know that without having a meeting set up, I wasn't getting past the security clearance.

Slowly, I glanced around the lobby trying to find a stairwell, freight elevator, or any other way to get up to the thirtieth floor where the interviews were being held. As if God had heard my silent prayer, I spotted a delivery girl coming through the front rotating doors and heading straight to the restroom.

"Bingo."

I channeled my inner spy as I made my way to the restroom, glad that there were only two closed stall doors when I entered. My nose immediately turned upward when I noticed the bag of food sitting on one of the sinks.

Disgusting. This is why I rarely order take out. Of course it was easy to order food to be delivered instead of cooking all of the time, but I never trusted food deliveries. The fact that the food currently sitting on the sink wasn't even mine still made me gag just thinking about all of the bacteria in the bathroom that was now contaminating the food.

One of the stalls opened and out stepped a businesswoman with a phone in one hand and laptop in the other. *How the hell did she even use the washroom with no free hands?* I considered myself a multi-tasker, but even I didn't understand that equation.

The businesswoman made quick work of washing her hands and exiting the restroom, leaving me alone with the delivery girl in the closed stall. When I heard the toilet flush, I only had a few seconds to figure out what I was going to say to her.

"Hello," she said, washing her hands.

Oh good, she's friendly. I can work with friendly. She was wearing an orange and yellow uniform with the words *Fly Wings* written on her T-shirt and a matching hat.

"Hello," I replied, pretending to touch up my lipstick. I'd worked at a wing place in high school, so I figured developing some commonality was the best place to start.

"I'm new to New York, so I haven't heard of *Fly Wings*, but I used to frequent a few wing places in my Tennessee hometown. Even worked at one for a while. Should I try *Fly Wings*?"

"Honestly," she said with a smile, "it's not worth the calories. There are way better wing places in the city. I'm only working here to save money for an apartment while I go to fashion design school."

"That's awesome. Nothing wrong with working to further your dream."

"Thanks." She dried her hands and frowned. "I just wished the uniform we had to wear wasn't so hideous. Every time I make a delivery to the tech company on the twentieth floor, the group that sits in the front of the office always make fun of me. I used to go to high school with a few of the guys and girls that intern there. I think they only place orders because they want to tease me."

I shook my head as I thought about how annoying some kids were. "I was teased a lot in high school, and even though it stopped by the time I went to college, I understand how you feel." I didn't want to deceive the young girl, but I had my own agenda as well. "You know, I happen to be work on the twentieth floor, too. I don't mind dropping off the food so that you don't have to go up there today."

Her eyes lit up. "Really? You'd do that for me?"

"Of course," I said with a shrug. "It's not a problem."

"Thank you." She gave me a hug before placing the bag of food in my hand. "Maybe you should wear this, too. Just so that they won't call *Fly Wings* and tell them that a random person delivered their food. They would totally do that to me."

I glanced down at the orange and yellow hat in her hand. "Sure. I can do that." I placed the hat on my head and tried not to cringe at the large cartoon bird. "I never did have a head that looked good in hats."

"You look fine," she told me after I put on the hat. "My name is Sadie by the way."

"Nice to meet you, Sadie." I extended my hand. "My name is Avery."

"Well, Avery, today you are my hero." When Sadie left the bathroom, there was an extra pep in her step.

Getting past security was a breeze once I told them I had food to deliver. Staying true to my word, I dropped off the food to the tech company on the twentieth floor. Although the receptionist took the food, the people at the nearby desks turned their heads to see who was delivering the food and looked disappointed to find me and not Sadie. *Brats.* If I hadn't been on a mission, I would have given them a quick lesson on bullying.

When I got back into the elevator and pressed the button to the thirtieth floor, my heart was beating out of my chest as I watched each floor light up. I was alone, which was a good thing because I had to give myself a pep talk.

"Now isn't the time to freeze up, Avery. You deserve this opportunity just as much as the next person."

To say I was nervous would be a huge understatement. I was beyond nervous. I wasn't even sure there was a word for what I felt. When the elevator doors swooshed open, I almost didn't step out of the elevator until a woman sitting at the front desk called out to me.

"Young lady, are you here to visit the gallery?"

"Um, yes. Yes, I am." I stepped off the elevator and was momentarily caught off guard to find the same woman I'd seen in the subway earlier.

I glanced around the immaculate space as I made my way to the desk. I'd read enough about Malakai Madden to know that his gallery that displayed his artwork and sculptures took up the entire thirtieth floor.

The older woman frowned. "I'm sorry, but the gallery is closed today. However, it will reopen tomorrow at 8 a.m."

I shook my head to clear my thoughts. "I'm sorry, I'm not actually here for the gallery. I'm here for—" I didn't get to finish the rest of my sentence as a man burst through a side door.

"Fuck him," the man said, pressing the button to the elevator.

The older woman stood from her seat. "Sir, you will watch your language."

The man looked so heated, I thought he would say something disrespectful, but instead, he huffed and got on the elevator.

"I'm sorry about that," she said to me as she fumbled around with some papers. "What did you say you were here for?"

"No apology necessary." I cleared my throat. "I'm here for the image consultant interview."

She stopped what she was doing. "I had six interviews scheduled today and two have already interviewed. The remaining four are currently waiting in the conference room. What is your name?"

"Avery Nightingale of The Nightingale Agency." I stood up straighter. "And if I'm being completely honest, the only reason I knew about this interview is because I overheard you on the phone this morning while I was on the subway."

She squinted her eyes. "I knew you looked familiar. I remember seeing you this morning as well." She surveyed me up and down. "You seem a bit young to have your own agency."

I smiled. "I get that a lot, ma'am. But I'm actually thirty-two years old."

She walked around her desk and observed me closer. "You're not from New York, are you?"

I nervously pushed my glasses farther up on my nose. "Um, no, ma'am. I'm not. But I assure you that I'm very good at what I do. All I ask is for a chance to interview for the position. My agency may be small, but I have some grand ideas that I think would really help Mr. Madden's image. I'm new to New York, so when I heard you on the subway, I knew I couldn't pass up the opportunity."

She wore a slight smirk on her face and in my gut, I knew that was a good sign. "I'll tell you what, Ms. Nightingale. You remind me a lot of myself when I was your age. My name is Ethel Woodstock." I accepted the outstretched hand. Her grip was firm, but welcoming. "I'll give you a chance to interview for the position. However, I must warn you that Mr. Madden is not easy to please. He's the best employer I've ever worked for, but over the past year, he's been through six previous image consultants who were unable to get the job done."

Job done? He's worked with some of the biggest PR agents and image consultants in the country. I'd done my research, so I already knew of a few of the agents he'd fired.

Every article I read just said they were let go due to undis-
closed differences, whatever the hell that meant. As if
reading my mind, she handed me a packet of information.

"The other candidates were able to spend a few days
reviewing this packet of information, so I suggest you brush
up on a much as you can in the next two hours. Each interview will be thirty minutes." She took a quick glance at my
attire. "The conference room is right through those double
doors. If you'd like to freshen up, the restroom is down the
hall to the right of the conference room."

"Thank you," I squealed. I was so excited that I couldn't
stop myself from giving her a quick hug regardless of how
unprofessional it may have seemed. Thankfully, she
returned my hug.

When I approached the conference room, the palms of
my hand grew sweaty at the sight of three men and one
woman waiting for their interview. Although Tennessee
was no New York, I'd worked with the best PR agency in
the state when I'd lived there. I'd gotten an internship
during my freshman year of college, which meant I had
fourteen years of experience in the industry.

I greeted the others that were in the room, but I might as
well have just kept my *hello* to myself. I received a smile
from one of the men and barely a glance of recognition from
the others.

I didn't let the dismissiveness bother me. I had a packet
of info to learn in two hours and I couldn't waste my time
being self-conscious about what the others thought of me.

One of the men in the room was called into the interview, and based off the fact that he left the room ten
minutes later, I assumed it hadn't gone well. My assumption
was proven correct when Ms. Woodstock entered the
conference room.

"Ladies and gentlemen, if I can have your attention for a moment." We all looked up from our notes and packet. "Mr. Madden has given me permission to prepare you all a little more for what to expect when you enter the room."

Ms. Woodstock took a seat at the head of the table before continuing. "As I mentioned to each of you when you arrived, Mr. Madden has not had the best of luck with finding the perfect image consultant for the job. Everyone in this room has been given an opportunity to change that. When you enter his office, you will find his personal assistant, the gallery manager, his business agent, and two of his most trusted advisors who also happen to be members of the Madden family. If you are uncomfortable with inter-viewing in front of a panel of individuals, then I suggest you get over it fast." She stood from her chair and smoothed down her skirt. "Good luck to each of you. We'll resume interviews in fifteen minutes."

After she left the room, I was still looking at the space she had recently vacated. The energy in the room was even more tense than it had been before. Putting myself out there wasn't easy, but I needed my business to be a success. I needed to prove to myself and others I'd left back in Tennessee that there wasn't anything I couldn't accomplish and they were wrong for doubting me. But trying to land one of the most high profile PR cases in the city right now? This may not have been the best idea after all.

FOUR

Avery

I glanced at the clock as the next interviewee was being called.

Come on, Avery. Focus. I wasn't the type to get nervous when I was confident in what I had to say, but I'd be lying to myself if I didn't admit that I was anxious to get this interview over with. Mainly because of the person in question.

I doubted there was anyone with a pulse who hadn't seen the private photo of Malakai Madden that went viral a year ago. I'd barely been able to look at anything else all day. I'd met some friends out for a drink the day it all went down and it had been the talk of the bar.

I'd followed Malakai Madden for years. On the day everything happened, I hadn't been on social media to see the news that he'd decided to stop playing the field and settle down, but it made sense why his exes and hopefuls alike had gone crazy on Twitter when he finally did make a statement.

A cough from one of the other candidates pulled me from my thoughts. I wasn't here to daydream. I was here to land Malakai Madden as a client. For the next hour and a half, I engrossed myself in the details in the packet. I was glad I'd already familiarized myself with what I'd read in the media because it made a lot of what was presented about his business and the reason he needed an image consultant make sense. Before long, I was the last candidate left.

"Ms. Nightingale, you're up." I assumed the guy who had been getting the candidates was the personal assistant, but I couldn't be sure.

His smile seemed friendly, but he appeared to be judging my outfit. "Are you going to remove that?" he asked as he opened the door to the office.

"Remove what?" I asked as I walked through the door. I didn't even hear what his response was because all the air was sucked from my lungs the moment my eyes landed on the group of people in the room. The energy crackled with expectation and the notion that this was an opportunity that was not to be fucked up. The man and woman sitting on the couch got my attention first.

The woman motioned for me to take a seat in the chair across from the sofa. I curled my fingers into a fist to keep myself from getting fidgety and listened as they were introduced as Mr. Madden's business agent, Paul Canton, and gallery manager, Serenity Taylor.

Next, the man who'd escorted me to the room introduced himself as Tyler Jeffrey, the personal assistant, and introduced two men who were seated in chairs adjacent from me as Malik and Crayson Madden. In my research, I'd noted that Malakai also had five brothers, but the pictures on the internet hadn't done these two justice.

Malik gave me a friendly smile while Crayson gave me an amused one. I would have speculated what he found so funny if I hadn't been introduced to the last person in the room next, Malakai Madden.

The moment those hazel eyes locked on me, my steps faltered. It made no damn sense for a man to look both sexy and sophisticated at the same time. He was wearing maroon pants, a beige blazer, and a navy button-up that would look mismatched on the average person, but on him, the colors just worked. One leg was crossed over another so that his foot rested on his knee giving me a good view of his stylish brown loafers.

A neatly trimmed beard decorated his mahogany dipped in cinnamon face, and although I liked beards, it was his hairstyle that had me squeezing my fists more. I loved running my hands through a man's hair, and Malakai's faded sides with soft curls on top had my palms itching. Pair that with some sexy suckable lips and I was damn near panting in that office.

"Nice to meet you all," I finally said to the room. I didn't trust myself to just address Malakai Madden and keep the longing out of my voice, so I kept my greeting simple.

"Thank you for coming," Malakai said. "As you know, the position I currently have open is for an image consultant. I must warn you that I've been burned a few times by consultants who didn't have my best interests at heart, so let me start by telling you about my expectations."

Expectations. That one word slipped from his mouth and slapped me against my thighs with need. Malakai Madden wasn't just anyone to me. He was one of my icons.

A man whose work I'd admired since he first got recognized when he was in high school. Only true artists or lovers of art knew everything he'd had to overcome to get to where he was today, and although I didn't know him personally, I felt like I did.

The timber of his voice was interesting to me because as he spoke, it was smooth, but also held a certain edge. I had the feeling that anything he said, he said with conviction regardless if he was confident in what he was saying or not.

His shoulders were broader than I thought they'd be, which meant all I wanted to do was climb on top of those broad shoulders and see how strong he really was. And I wouldn't even climb him like a damn tree. I'd climb him like a mountain. A mountain took longer to climb. A mountain had twists and turns that you couldn't prepare for. A mountain could hold the weight of a thousand trees and Malakai looked like he'd be up for the challenge.

I shook my head at the thought. *Get a grip, Nightingale. This isn't the time or place.*

"Do you understand?"

I nodded. "Yes, I do."

"Great." He shuffled through some papers on the desk. "I don't seem to have your resume."

"Oh, right." I glanced around the room for my messenger bag and realized I'd left it in the conference room. "I don't have it with me, but I'd be happy to tell you about my experience."

He frowned. "Okay." He sat back in his desk chair. "I'm a bit unconventional, but let's start with why you believe your experience makes you the perfect person."

Perfect person? Perfect person romantically? "The perfect person," I repeated aloud.

He squinted his eyes. "Exactly. The perfect person for me to hire as my image consultant."

Duh, Nightingale. This is an interview. What the hell did you think he meant? "Oh, right."

"That's the second time you've said that."

"Said what?" I asked. Then it dawned on me. "Oh, right." *Shit. I need to stop saying 'Oh, right'.* I opened my mouth prepared to wow him with my experience and ideas I had to improve his image, but no words came out. None. Zilch.

I adjusted myself in my seat and tried again. "Well, I'm the perfect person for the job, because I fit perfectly with what you need in a consultant." I almost gagged at my own words. *What the hell are you saying, Nightingale?*

"Uh." Malakai's eyes widened as if he couldn't believe that was my response. I didn't dare look around the room, but I was sure the snort I heard was from Crayson Madden.

I stood up with some hope that standing would help me get my shit together. "What I meant to say was that I am perfectly perfect because of the experience I have. Fifteen years and three months of experience to be exact." *That wasn't any better. You're destroying this interview.*

Malakai squeezed the bridge of his nose. "I'm sorry, but I don't think we should continue with this interview."

"But I'm perfect," I all but yelled, followed by a chain of words that even I couldn't make out. As much as I hated for my mom to be right, she'd always said that I had verbal diarrhea whenever I got too nervous. Of course, she'd made that assumption after my fifth-grade school play in which I went to say my lines, froze, and then recited every line I had in the entire play in a matter of seconds. Every now and then, my dad would join in and tease me about going into a career as an auction announcer since I could speak so fast.

"I'm sure you're perfect for some client," Malakai said. "Although, at the moment, I can't think of what type of client that may be." *Rude.* "But thank you for ... I'm not sure what I'm thanking you for, but the interview is over. Tyler will see you out."

I slouched a little where I stood even though I couldn't blame him. I'd botched that interview so bad, that even I wouldn't have listened anymore after my fifth mention of the word *perfect.* I was almost out the door when I heard my name.

"Ms. Nightingale."

Lord have mercy. The way he said my last name made my knees quiver and I was pretty sure I drooled a little. I hadn't realized he hadn't addressed me by name since I'd arrived until he just did.

Mustering up all of the dignity I had left, I turned back around to face him. "Yes, Mr. Madden?"

His eyes made their way to the top of my head. I was sure the next words out of his mouth were going to sound even sexier than the way he said my name. However, my lust bubble was popped when he asked, "Is there a reason you're wearing a Fly Wings hat?"

Oh, crap! I quickly removed the hat and fluffed out my curls, which had been stuffed under the hat.

"That's what I asked you before," Tyler whispered to me. I hadn't even known when he'd gotten so close, but I could tell by the look in his eyes that he felt sorry for me.

A part of me felt like I should say something else to try and redeem myself. Or at explain the stupid hat. Instead, I let Tyler escort me out.

"Honey, are you okay?" Tyler asked once the office door was closed.

"I'm fine," I lied, noticing for the first time how well he

was dressed in his royal blue pants and grey button-up. When we reached the conference room, I noticed my messenger bag. "I just thought I would have killed that interview instead of doing whatever it is you call what I just did."

Tyler nodded his head. "Yeah, it was pretty painful to watch. I thought for sure you were the one."

I raised an eyebrow. "One for what?"

"The *perfect* person for the job," he said with a laugh. "I had good vibes about you."

As good as that sounded to my ears, it also hurt a little. "Thanks, but unless I can turn back time and redo my interview, I officially lost my chance."

"Maybe you can." Tyler glanced up and down at my outfit. "Did you bring a sweater with you?"

"Yes." I reached in my messenger bag and pulled out my white sweater.

"Do you mind?" he asked. I shrugged, unsure what he was asking, but knew I felt comfortable around him regardless. He fixed the collar of my white blouse and tied my white sweater around my waist so that it was loosely draped over my hips and hid the coffee stain I'd forgotten about.

Going with the flow he'd set, I took out a couple of my bobby pins and twisted my hair to the side, fluffing out my curls a bit more. Next, I applied a coat of soft red lipstick, while Tyler cleaned off my glasses before placing them back on my face.

"There," he said, observing his work. "Now you're ready to head back in there and wow him like you'd planned on doing before."

"Thank you for this."

He shrugged. "Don't mention it. Just go in there and impress my boss."

There was an extra pep in my step as I walked back to the office ready to prove to Malakai Madden that I was the image consultant he'd been waiting for.

FIVE

Malakai

"Well, today was a shit show," I said aloud after Tyler escorted the last candidate out the room. Had anyone told me a year ago that it was easier to become famous overnight than find a decent image consultant, I would have called them on their bullshit.

My brothers walked up to my desk as Serenity and Paul got engrossed in a separate conversation about the upcoming party I was having to release some new art pieces.

"It wasn't that bad," Malik said optimistically. "The interviews may not have been what you expected, but at least I was here when Antoine arrived."

In the middle of the interviews, the last image consultant I'd had to fire, Antoine Walters, had arrived demanding that I give him his job back or he would sue. Since Malik was a private investigator, I'd had him start investigating Antoine months ago when I learned that instead of doing his job, he'd been using me to make connections and further his own agenda. Even if that meant selling pictures of me to local news outlets.

I'd told Malik that there was a chance Antoine would show up to the interviews and I wanted him there just in case. Malik had just arrived on a red-eye flight, and when Antoine showed up making demands, I slapped him with some legal demands of my own.

"I disagree with Malik," Crayson said. "It was all pretty damn painful to watch." Crayson was the jokester of my brothers and never one to hold his tongue. Growing up, we always thought that he would never get his act together long enough to have a real job or business. However, he'd shocked us all when he said he was opening his own cigar lounge. Honestly, I thought that he would go out of business within the first year due to lack of discipline, but not only had he been thriving for the past eight years, he'd also opened another location in the area.

"Especially that last one," Crayson continued. "Makes no sense that a woman that attractive would be horrible at speaking. Especially in the PR field."

With both Crayson and I living in New York, we often discussed important business together, so I'd asked him to come and give me his input. Sugar coating wasn't even in Crayson's vocabulary.

"She was nervous," Malik countered. "It probably didn't help that you kept laughing at her."

Crayson held out his arms in defense. "I wasn't laughing at her. I was laughing at the *Fly Wings* hat she was wearing. I got the feeling that she hadn't remembered she had it on. Then I was curious why she was wearing it in the first place. Maybe she works there?"

I shook my head. "Not sure. But I could tell she's not

from New York. It was evident by the way she carried herself. Even though she was nervous, instead of being stiff, she seemed relaxed. Instead of acting like the world owed her something, she appeared to be thankful for the opportunities placed before her. Instead of being stone-faced, she smiled a lot." *And damn if that smile didn't get to me.*

` When Ethel had handed me a piece of paper in between interviews, the only words written on the paper were *Avery Nightingale of The Nightingale Agency. Last interview for the day.* Today marked the third set of inter-views I'd had in the past couple weeks to find the right image consultant, and once again, I'd ended the day feeling defeated.

Even if Ms. Nightingale would have given a great inter-view, I'm not sure I would have hired her for the position. There was something about her that made me pause what-ever I was thinking or doing and just watch her. Listen to her rambling. Take in her cheerfulness and beauty. How could any man get shit done with that type of distraction around?

"You're thinking about her, aren't you?"

I blinked out of my fog and looked to Crayson. "Sorry, what?"

"Bruh, you know what I mean," he said with a knowing smile. "Even though her interview was terrible, you're still thinking about that brown-skinned honey who just left your office. She's your type."

"Man, please. She's not my type." I almost added the fact that I hadn't been thinking about her, but there was no point in lying that much.

"I hate to agree with Crayson on any damn thing," Malik interjected, "but he's right. She's your type."

I was about to deny the claim, when the topic of conversation walked through my office door without knocking.

"Mr. Madden, I want a second chance."

"Uh." My mouth parted slightly.

"Here you go." She walked up to my desk and handed me a folder. "This is my portfolio and resume that you requested earlier. I apologize for my lack of professionalism, but I promise you, I truly am good at what I do."

I glanced around the room and noticed the hopeful look in everyone's eyes, especially Tyler's who'd entered the office behind her. They didn't even know her, yet it was clear they wanted me to give her another chance.

"Okay, Ms. Nightingale. Please continue."

Her smile slowly brightened her face and hit me right in the gut. *This is not a good idea.* She'd changed her hair, and since she'd discarded the hat, I got a healthy view of her elegant neck and luscious brown curls.

"Mr. Madden, first let me jump right in and start by saying that what happened to you a year ago was unfortunate and I wouldn't wish that type of invasion of privacy on anyone."

I almost smiled at the sincerity in her voice, but kept my face neutral.

"But if I'm being honest, part of the reason you haven't been able to change your image is because you fail to acknowledge what really needs to change."

Say what? "I can assure you, Ms. Nightingale, that I've acknowledged what needs to change. Not that it's any of your business *yet* since this is just an interview."

"That's precisely why it's my business," she interrupted. "But continue."

I adjusted the collar of my shirt, refusing to admit that she was getting to me. "I've taken large strides to assure that

I'm not in the public eye with a woman, otherwise, the media will have a field day. I also ended any casual female relationship I had a year ago. Some even before Twitter had a field day."

"And that's part of the problem," she said, lightly pacing the room in a way that demanded everyone's attention. "Whether they be single, married, or bi-sexual, women around the world want to have sex with you, Mr. Madden, and in a statement that I assume was written by the first publicist or consultant you hired, you told the world that you indeed wanted to find a woman to marry and were done playing the field."

"Which I am," I told her.

"But you're not." She raised a finger in the air. "What's the one thing that all of those women who tweeted about you and continue to talk about you on social media today really want?"

"Uh ..." I was sure I knew the answer, but I didn't know what she was getting at.

"They want you," she said. "They want to follow your every move. They want to marry you. They want to have sex with you. And if they can't have you, any woman with a romantic bone in her body wants to see you have a relationship of substance and find the wife that you claim to be looking for. How can you find the one when you aren't even looking?"

I shook my head. "But I thought the purpose of cleaning up my act was to avoid having any relationships in the public eye so that the media would lose interest and I would be able to find the right woman for me?"

"Wrong," she replied. "Right now, the media and all of your followers are assuming that instead of discontinuing to have casual relationships, you've decided to continue doing what you've always done, only more discreetly. In this day and age, society is nosey and people want to see what you're doing. Especially on your level. Your artwork and high-profile clientele may have gotten you noticed by many, but it's your looks, style, and personality that got you over five-hundred thousand followers. Instead of avoiding the media, you need to show everyone that you have re-branded yourself and are indeed still trying to find that wife you claim to want."

All I could do was stare at her in disbelief. Up until now, every publicist or image consultant I'd come into contact with had gone the route of staying out of the public's eye, especially with a woman. Yet, she was standing before me basically saying that all those before her were wrong where I was concerned. Her view was refreshing, and as much as I hated to admit it, it made more sense than anything I'd heard in months.

I was eating up her words and impressed by how much work she'd already put into a position that wasn't hers yet. "What would be the first thing you think I should do to take a step in the direction you're suggesting?"

Her lips curled to the side in a smirk as she took two steps closer to me. "Like I said before, I have over fifteen years of experience and I've followed your case closely. The ideas and plan I have for you are unconventional, but I believe in my work and more importantly, I believe in you and your desire to change your image."

Her voice seemed to grow lower, or maybe it was just my mind hoping her velvet voice had dropped to an even sexier octave. "If you hire me, Mr. Madden, I promise to execute my plan to the best of my ability. You've gone the route of hiring a large PR agency. You've already worked with enough well-known consultants who I get the feeling didn't have your best interests at heart. But make no mistake, I am hungry to prove that my small agency can swim with the big fish. So all I'm asking for is a chance to prove my value by helping you rebrand yourself. If you take a chance on me, you won't be disappointed."

I sat there, dumbfounded by everything she'd just presented to me. *Disappointed?* Something told me there was no way for her to ever disappoint me and that notion was a scary one that had the angel on my shoulder telling me not to hire her no matter how great she'd pitched herself just now.

"I'm sure you have to talk with your team about all of the candidates, so I'll escort myself out. Thank you for giving me a second chance."

Second chance? Hell, I'd give her a third, fourth, fifth, or six chance if she smiled at me the way she'd been doing since she'd arrived.

She turned to the door, forcing me to test my self-control by not looking at the sway of her hips as she walked.

"You're in trouble," Crayson whispered to me. He was right on the money. Hiring a woman I was attracted to was a big fat no in my book. Unfortunately, the devil on my other shoulder had decided to show up to the party.

You know you should hire her, he taunted. *You want her too badly not to hire her.* "Shit," I swore aloud, not caring if everyone in the office could hear me.

"My girl!" Tyler gave her a high-five as she exited. He turned to me. "Sorry, boss," he said sheepishly. "But she killed that."

Yep, she'd killed it. And I was in some deep trouble because even before Avery Nightingale fully made it out of my office, I knew what I was going to do.

SIX

Avery

"I can't believe it," I exclaimed as I downed my entire cup of water as if it were a shot of tequila, before slamming the glass down on the bar.

"Easy there on the H2O," my friend, Jordyn, told me as she refilled the empty glass with more water. Jordyn and I had only known each other for six months, but we immediately clicked. She was the proud owner of Sweet Baby Jay's, a bar known for pairing unique drinks with tasty treats guaranteed to tease your pallet.

"He offered me a job," I said for the third time today. "He actually hired me as his image consultant."

"That's because he knows a good hire when he sees one. And, you my friend, are going to be listed in the papers as the woman who accomplished what consultants before her had failed to do."

I'd just gotten the call an hour ago from Ms. Woodstock

letting me know that I was hired and was to come into the office to sign the paperwork tomorrow. I'd immediately walked down from my apartment to my friend's bar that took up the entire first level. It was only around one in the afternoon, so although Sweet Baby Jay's had a good number of people there, it really livened up after four for happy hour.

I glanced at my phone to see if Tyler had texted that he and Serenity were on their way. Right after I'd received the call from Ms. Woodstock, Tyler had messaged me and asked if they could meet me for lunch. Supposedly, they wanted to chat before I started tomorrow.

Back in Tennessee, I'd always enjoyed hanging out with co-workers, so it hadn't taken long for me to message him back and suggest Jordyn's bar. Plus, I was curious why they wanted to chat before I'd even started working with them.

"Are you nervous?" Jordyn asked, getting my attention.

"Me? Nervous? Not at all."

She just smiled and continued drying glasses. Jordyn knew me well enough to know I was being sarcastic. Was I nervous? Hell yeah. Who wouldn't be in my situation? I had a lot to prove, and no matter how confident I'd seemed yesterday when I'd interviewed, I'd been a nervous wreck when I'd walked back into Malakai Madden's office.

The only thing that had calmed my nerves was the fact that everyone in the room, him included, had given me their undivided attention. I could tell I'd piqued his interest, and once I'd planted a few seeds pertaining to my plans to improve his image, I'd gone from the worst person he'd probably ever interviewed to a potential candidate.

"I think your friends are here."

I glanced over my shoulder just as Tyler and Serenity were coming through the front door. Both were dressed incredibly well with Tyler sporting some modern beige slacks with a teal button-up and bow tie, while Serenity was wearing a flowy navy dress and matching heels.

"How did you guess that was them?"

"They have that New York Manhattan swag," Jordyn answered. "We tend to get more of the Brooklyn or Harlem type of crowd."

It was true. Both looked as though they'd walked off the pages of a magazine. As they approached us, I introduced them to Jordyn.

I pointed to a high-table in the corner that I'd already decided offered the best sunlight and privacy for us to meet. Once we were situated, Tyler wasted no time getting down to the reason behind their impromptu visit.

"The reason we wanted to meet with you before you start is simple," he said. "Even though we barely know you, we already like you."

"And we want you to succeed," Serenity added with a smile. "So we figured if we gave you a couple tips, maybe it would help with your position."

I squinted my eyes, a little confused as to why they felt like I needed so much help. I mean, damn, I may have just started my business, but I wasn't clueless.

Tyler rolled his eyes. "What my homegirl is trying to say is that it's not you we're worried about. It's Double M."

My eyebrows rose. "Double who?"

"Malakai Madden. AKA, Double M. My nickname for him changes depending on my mood."

Jordyn briefly interrupted the conversation when she dropped off waters. I was trying to figure out what the glare was all about until I heard Tyler say, "Well, don't you look tasty."

I laughed even though it only earned a second glare

from Jordyn. Was my friend extremely beautiful with her flawless brown skin and chic curly hairdo? Absolutely. Did the sleeve of tattoos on her arm and pin-up style wardrobe gain her a lot of attention? Hell yeah. Did she appreciate the lust-filled glances she received from men daily? Not one iota.

Jordyn lifted her fist. "My hand is mighty tasty, too. Care to find out?"

Tyler raised up his hands in defense. "Damn, chica, I'm scared of you. It's not even like that. I appreciate a woman with her own style. That's all."

Jordyn ground her teeth without saying anything in response.

"Don't let him get to you," Serenity said apologetically. "Tyler's mouth is always getting him in trouble, but it's all good, sis. He bats for the other team anyway."

Tyler shot Jordyn a sneaky smile. I wanted to tell him Jordyn wasn't the type of woman to play with, but Jordyn made that clear when she leaned closer to Tyler. "I love a good joke as much as anyone, but if you plan on dishing it out, you better be ready to take it." She looked at me and Serenity. "If you need anything besides water, let me know." She shot Tyler one more warning before she left.

Tyler placed his hand over his heart. "I think I just found my new bestie."

Serenity rolled her eyes, giving me the distinct impression that Tyler had a lot of besties.

"Anywho, what were we talking about?" He snapped his fingers. "Oh, right. We were discussing Mr. McGrouch. Like I was saying before, we aren't worried about you being able to handle the job. In fact, you won over everyone in the room during your second interview."

"We're worried about you being run off because

Malakai has been burned so many times," Serenity added. "I've been managing his art gallery for a while now, and he's more jaded than I've ever known him to be."

First name basis? Sad puppy dog eyes of pity? If I didn't know better, I'd say they knew one another personally. "How so?"

"I've known Malakai since we were kids," Serenity replied. "Although he may appear to be easy-going, he likes things in order. Everything has a place and there is a place for everything. This Twitter mess has turned his life upside down."

I tried my best to mask my curiosity, but I knew I'd failed at doing so when Tyler said, "They never dated if that's what you're wondering." He smirked. "My girl has had her eye on one of the Madden triplets since they were kids."

I took a sip of my water, wanting to know more, but trying not to pry since they barely knew me.

Serenity began shaking her head before she even spoke. "Don't listen to Tyler. I've known all of the Madden brothers since I was a kid, but I went to school with Malakai's younger brothers ... the triplets. Caden, Crayson, and—"

"Carter," Tyler said in a dreamy voice. Serenity swatted him on the arm.

"I do not sound like that when I say his name."

"Yes, you do, sweetie." Tyler lifted his hand to his mouth to whisper to me even though I was pretty sure Serenity could still hear us. "Carter is the quiet, brooding Madden brother who you rarely hear about. Word is, he's elite military, but like I said, we don't really talk about him."

"Did you date?" I asked. Since Tyler had already spilled the beans, I figured I might as well throw in a question.

However, I almost took it back when she stumbled over her words.

"We didn't. I mean, we did. But not like that. We weren't. He wasn't. I wasn't." Her shoulders slumped a little. "It's complicated."

Tyler glanced at me. "It's painful to watch, right?" He placed a hand on Serenity's shoulder. "We get it, girl. Y'all dated, but you want to keep that shit on the hush because he fucked up. Or maybe you fucked up." He squinted his eyes at her. "Or did you find out he swung more my way than yours?"

"Stop speculating," Serenity said, shaking her head. "None of the above and none of your business. Can we get back to what we came here for?"

Tyler gave her a knowing look, but changed the subject. "Lunch is almost over anyway, so we can."

"We think he needs a consultant like you," Serenity stated, diving right back into the main topic and catching me off guard.

I studied the hopeful look in their eyes. "Although I appreciate the vote of confidence, why me?"

They glanced at one another before focusing on me. I shouldn't have been nervous about the answer, but I couldn't help the butterflies that surfaced when Serenity said, "Because you're different than any of the previous people he's hired, and even though it was a quick interview, he seemed comfortable with you. He seemed to trust you."

"Sometimes, it takes someone unexpected to come into someone's life and change it," Tyler added. "Although you were wearing that god-awful hat, I peeped you were different. M&M is a great boss and we want what's best for him."

Serenity's eyes softened. "We don't want to put pressure on you, but we were soaking in everything you said during your interview. We have faith that you'll prove to be the right hire, but if you're ever uncertain about anything, feel free to ask us or Malakai. He appreciates honesty and being up-front about things."

As Tyler and Serenity continued to talk to me about Malakai Madden, surprisingly, it only made me more hyped to prove that the right person had been hired for the job. Even if there was a tiny part of me that was nervous to work for a man I'd idolized for so long.

Avery

TOMORROW CAME QUICKER than I'd anticipated, and after the afternoon I'd had the day before getting the inside scoop on what to expect working for Malakai Madden, I'd spent all night prepping for my first day.

Now, I was on the elevator headed to the office, mentally hyping myself for what was yet to come. *You got this shit,* I chanted in my head. *When you're a boss chick, you don't need to prove yourself. Your skill is proven in your work ethic. So kill it today and you'll set the standard high.*

I'd been saying the last few sentences repeatedly like a broken record. I needed the words to sink in. Since I had to do paperwork first, I had a few hours before my scheduled meeting with Mr. Madden, but that didn't mean I didn't want to be over-prepared for that meeting.

"Hello, Ms. Woodstock," I greeted as soon as I got off the elevator and arrived at the front desk. "Nice to see you again."

I glanced to my left and noticed that the gallery was open today. I really wanted to check it out, but there would be time for that later.

"Ms. Nightingale, nice to see you as well." She stood and reached for a packet from her desk. "I'm so glad you're here a little early. There has been a slight change of plans. Instead of filling out your paperwork now, Mr. Madden would like to speak with you first."

Say what? I froze, hoping that I'd heard her wrong. Clearing my throat, I asked, "Did you say that Mr. Madden needs to see me now?"

"Yes, dear. I'll show you to his office and we'll work on your paperwork afterward."

Shit. "Okay, sounds good." For the first time, I noticed how long the hallway was to his office as I followed Ms. Woodstock. Most of the floor was dedicated to the gallery, but I noticed a few people in the office who I assumed were the team of people who reported to Serenity.

When we reached Mr. Madden's office, Ms. Woodstock knocked and waited for his response that we could come in.

"Ms. Nightingale has arrived. After you've finished your meeting, we will continue with her paperwork."

I noticed Tyler first. He was smiling when he walked over to me and lowered his head to my ear.

"Good luck. I know you're going to slay your first day."

"Thanks, Ty," I whispered back.

He waved his fingers in front of me and his nails looked better groomed than mine. "Already using nicknames, I like it. I'll leave you to it." He cocked his head toward the direction where Mr. Madden was standing next to the window gazing down on the city.

Although he wasn't looking my way yet, my body didn't seem to understand that. I glanced down at my navy blouse and teal skirt, making sure my clothes were in order after the chill that had just ricocheted through me. *That's so weird.* I was no virgin to the way it felt to be attracted to a man. I'd had my fair share of *excuse-me-while-I-pick-my-jaw-off-the-ground* moments. But I'd never been the type to react to a man by simply walking into the same room. Especially when he wasn't even directing his attention to me.

But typically, I wasn't staring at a sexy man with an ass like that. Round. Firm. Could fill a pair of pants like nobody's business. I tried my best not to bite my bottom lip at the thought of sinking my teeth into his juicy ass. Some women liked legs. Others liked a nice smile and strong jawline. There were a few who maybe liked feet. Lots that liked nice abs and shoulders. But me? I was a sucker for a nice ass.

The light click of the door pulled me from my daydream and reminded me that admiring my client's ass was not what he was paying me to do. Which was difficult since he still hadn't turned around to face me.

"Welcome to Malakai Madden Studios." His voice was as smooth as red velvet, and since we were the only two people in the room, I was able to truly listen to the different vibrations they displayed even though he'd only said five words.

"I'm excited to be here and appreciate the opportunity."

"While I'm thankful for your appreciation, that won't be enough to get you through this job."

Um, what? "I understand that and I believe I offer a different perspective to your situation."

"You made that much clear in your interview," he said. "But I've heard this all before, so it's only fair that I tell you I'm not yet convinced that you're the right image consultant for me, but I'm willing to give this a try."

It took all of my energy not to smack my tongue over the front of my teeth at his comment. I'd faced this before, so I knew what it was. Clients who'd been burned before and are apprehensive to put their trust in me so they rather voice their doubt than their hopes.

I didn't care because he was right, I hadn't proved myself yet. However, little did Mr. Madden know, I didn't scare easily.

"Well, my job would be a lot easier if you actually looked my way and gave me eye contact instead of out the window."

I briefly closed my eyes as soon as the words left my mouth. *What the hell, Avery? You're supposed to demand attention discreetly, not tell off your client on your first day.*

I opened my eyes to apologize and almost stumbled when my gaze collided with his. Beyoncé may have had all of us singing "Drunk in Love" years ago with a bottle of rosé in one hand and our girls chanting along, but standing there staring into Malakai Madden's eyes were the true definition of a drunken gaze and I was getting more intoxicated the longer his rich hazel eyes held mine.

"I understand your hesitation to place your trust in me," I said, breaking the silence. "But until you do, we won't be able to get very far in cleaning up your image. I'm not them, and although I hate to think that other consultants did something to earn your distrust, you have to move forward so that I can do my job."

His brown-cinnamon facial features softened—the only indication that he'd heard me since he still hadn't spoken. I didn't want to openly observe him, but I took a few moments to soak him in while he silently decided if I was worth any more of his time.

He was wearing beige, slim-fitted pants and a green and

beige patterned shirt, giving me this afro-centric vibe that had me wanting to pull out my phone and play a neo-soul song to fill the silence. Malakai Madden had that type of natural swag that many men tried to emulate and failed.

"I apologize," he said, catching me off guard. "It's been a rough few months, but I truly am glad that I hired you." He motioned to the chair opposite his desk.

"The reason I asked to speak with you as soon as you arrived is because I wanted to give you a little more insight into what happened with the last consultant I hired. I hope that's not a problem."

"Of course not." I placed my bag and purse on the chair beside me and accepted a sheet of paper he passed me.

"This is Antoine Walters, the man I had to fire a month ago."

I studied the photo. "I remember him. He was here the day I interviewed and was cursing all the way to the elevator."

Mr. Madden shook his head. "I'm not surprised. We didn't part on the best of terms, and he's always been ... expressive."

I scanned the sheet, my eye catching on words like theft and investigation.

"Long story short, a few months ago, some of my artwork showed up missing. I ran an investigation and found that Antoine had been stealing some of my artwork and selling it, keeping the profits for himself."

I shook my head. "That's unfortunate and disappointing."

"That's not all." Looking up from the sheet, I noticed the exhaustion in his eyes that I hadn't noticed previously. "Since he knew my schedule, he also took photos of me and was selling them to local media outlets. The pictures weren't risqué, but it was an invasion of privacy. Early on, I had a feeling he was the type to name drop and further his own personal connections, but I didn't know how badly he was screwing me over. And he's not the first to do this."

My eyes widened. "This has happened to you multiple times?"

"Not this particular situation, but I've worked with six previous consultants who didn't work out. Before Antoine, there was Josh and Pete. Before that Cynthia J, Rachel, and Ashley."

"Cynthia J is pretty well known," I said, thinking about the New York consultants I'd researched before moving here.

"She is and she's great at what she does. Except where I'm concerned." He adjusted the collar of his shirt, making me even more curious as to what she'd done. I was going to start guessing reasons why thinking about her made him uncomfortable when he said, "On some nights, I sleep in one of the spare offices that I had designed for late nights where I may be creating and couldn't make it home. Early on when she'd started, she'd propositioned me on several occasions and I thought I'd made it clear that this was strictly business. Then, one night she'd had too much to drink and came to the office, found me sleeping, and I awoke to find her in ... less than appropriate attire."

"Oh." My imagination filled in the rest. "I see."

He rubbed his forehead. "After that incident and me rejecting her advances, she quit."

I squinted my eyes. "I thought I read somewhere that she was fired?"

"She wanted to paint this ugly picture of me because she was hurt," he explained. "I'm not sure why she wanted everyone to believe that, but I was truly trying to get over her advances and focus on the reason she was hired. I'm not even going to go into the reasons the others didn't work out, but a similar situation happened with Rachel and with Pete."

I raised an eyebrow. "You mean Rachel *and* Pete both made advances toward you?"

He nodded his head. His voice low when he replied, "Yeah. There's more, but I won't get into it. However, I will tell you that these circumstances changed the way I must approach this partnership. As your client, I need to make sure that our relationship remains professional and that you won't feed into the social media craze as others before you failed to do."

I let out a breath and took a long blink, torn between wanting to commiserate with him, yet unable to stop the image of his dick that flashed across the back of my eyelids.

My mind was still trying to get the appetizing picture out of my head when I answered, "I understand. Strictly professional. I want to assure you that you won't have to worry about the same thing happening with me that happened with previous consultants."

His eyes studied mine, neither of us saying anything for a few seconds. When he finally nodded to acknowledge my response, I found myself nodding along with him. He kept his gaze trained on me, but the air around us seemed thick with an awareness I couldn't quite place. Was it annoyance? A warning? Sexual tension? Maybe all three mixed together?

The Malakai Madden fan in me wanted it to be the latter, and for that reason, I couldn't blame the others who had failed to put their personal feelings aside. However, the businesswoman in me knew that sex or thoughts of sex only complicated matters, so I shouldn't even entertain the idea that he felt the same sexual pull that I did.

The next words out of his mouth were barely above a whisper, and had I not been paying close attention to his every move, I would have missed him repeating, "Strictly professional." Based off the way he said the words, I couldn't tell if he was saying it more for my benefit ... or his.

SEVEN

Malakai

Four days, five hours, and twenty-seven minutes. That was how long I'd been working with Ms. Nightingale and trying to convince myself that hiring her was the right decision.

It wasn't as hard of a decision as I was making it out to be because professionally, she fit in perfectly with the team. She wouldn't have to be in the office all of the time, but Tyler had suggested she be in for the next couple weeks to get familiar with me and the business. I had wanted to say no, but it had actually been a good idea and something that the other consultants hadn't done.

Not even a week and she already had everyone wrapped around her finger, and even the temporary gallery employees often walked over to the side of the floor with the offices looking for Ms. Nightingale to take her to lunch or drinks after work.

She'd also scheduled two appearances for me at a boys

and girls club in Brooklyn and another in Harlem next week so that some good publicity could circulate about me. Apparently, they had some pretty great art programs and the directors were both excited to have a professional artist visit with the kids. It had been a while since I was around kids, so I was looking forward to it.

There was a light knock on the open door. "Mr. Madden, are you ready for me?"

I looked up from my laptop to the conference entryway, my eyes landing on a chestnut almond-shaped pair in black-rimmed glasses that had invaded their way into my mind all week. Hence, why I'd been struggling to convince myself that hiring her had been the right move.

I'm ready for you in more ways than you probably realize. "Yes, please come in, Ms. Nightingale."

She'd asked to meet with me yesterday, but the flattering skirt she'd been wearing had made it hard for me to keep my eyes off her legs, so I'd declined. I was a leg man. Always had been. And I couldn't remember the last time I'd seen a pair as sexy as hers.

She took a seat opposite me at the table, and since I hadn't seen her yet this morning, I couldn't have prepared myself for how she looked in a slim-fitted peach dress. Her physical features seemed softer. Curvier. I cursed myself for letting Ms. Woodstock talk me into choosing a glass table for the conference room instead of the black one I'd been set on getting. I could see every move she made under the table.

She cleared her throat and crossed her legs, the dress sliding farther up her thighs as she adjusted herself in the seat. *Fuck me.* I was never getting through this meeting. My dick jumped as if to say, "Serves your dumb ass right for deciding to go over a year without giving me any female attention."

I slightly spread my legs, giving him a chance to breathe and hoping he calmed the fuck down, and realized that if he kept acting up, he was going to get us both in trouble.

"Thank you for meeting with me," she said, her glossed lips opening and closing in a way that shouldn't have even been seductive, but it was.

"No problem. What did you want to talk about?" The sly smile that crossed her face made me pause. "I'm not sure I like that sneaky look."

Placing her hands in front of her, she laced her fingers together. The silver feather ring on her pointer finger caught my attention. Besides earrings, it was the only piece of jewelry she was wearing. *I wonder if she knows the current watercolor painting I'm working on is a feather?* Not likely since no one knew of the painting.

"Before we start, can you promise me that you will keep an open mind?"

I quirked an eyebrow. "I'm not sure I like where this is headed."

She shook her head. "How about I just dive in?"

I shouldn't have been watching her chest heave up and down as she took a deep breath but I couldn't help myself.

"When I interviewed, I mentioned that I had a great, albeit unconventional, plan to help improve your image. I know your first instinct once I tell you what that plan is will be to decline doing what I suggest, but I want to remind you that you've already had six previous consultants, so you've already had a lot of trial and error with conventional tactics."

It took a lot to make me nervous, and it wasn't that she necessarily made me nervous, but rather, she was so certain I would reject her idea without realizing that she wasn't easy for me to reject. Despite my pull toward her, I wasn't doing shit if it was too far out of my character.

In my bones, I knew I wasn't going to like what she had to suggest and that assumption was proven true when she said, "I want you to choose five women to date and do a series of live videos on Twitter."

I stared at her. "I'm sorry, but it sounded like you just suggested I go on dates with several different women and do live videos on Twitter. The same social media platform that caused this mess in the first damn place."

"That's exactly what I'm suggesting." She bent down to her bag and pulled out a couple folders, handing one to me. "Have you ever heard of Periscope?"

I shook my head.

She opened both folders and pointed to the short paragraph in the front. "Periscope is a live video streaming app and was acquired by Twitter a few years ago before they had a chance to launch. Now, of course you can go on Twitter and post live videos with a click of the button, but what I want to do is create your own Periscope account and have a regular schedule of live videos from you."

"My own series of live videos?"

She nodded her head. "Exactly."

"Why Periscope and not YouTube or something else?"

She pulled out the next sheet of paper. "A lot of frequent users say that Facebook, YouTube, and Instagram are actually better with live videos. However, Twitter is your biggest reach. Twitter followers love Malakai Madden and whether their reasons be because of your artwork or your relationship status, you've become a public figure that the Twitter audience wants to follow."

"I don't know about this." I skimmed through the section of my Twitter information. "What would I even go live about? You can't expect me to actually talk about my dates honestly to the world."

She smiled that sly smile of hers again. "Have you ever heard of Dr. William Walker? He's pretty well-known in New York."

I ran through popular names of New Yorkian doctors and came up blank. "What is he the doctor of?"

She turned to the next sheet in the packet of info. "Dr. William Walker is most well-known for being a love and relationship expert. He's helped numerous people find love and helped even more couples stay together."

I snapped my fingers. "Oh right. Didn't he have a television show for a short while? And now, I tend to see him doing more online counseling ..." My voice trailed off and my jaw dropped.

Although I was hoping she wasn't thinking along the lines that my mind had carried me, I couldn't hide my shock at her knowing look when she mouthed, "Exactly."

I dropped the folder to the table. "You've got to be shitting me."

"I shit you not." She pointed to a paragraph on the paper. "You haven't dated anyone in over a year, and after you made that declaration about being serious in your pursuit to find a wife, you haven't been seen with a woman in public. Therefore, I've spoken with one of the top matchmakers in the industry to find you the perfect five women to date. And I've also spoken to Dr. William Walker about partnering with you to go live with him after each date so that the public can get to know the real Malakai Madden and the man behind the dick pic."

I raised a curious eyebrow as her eyes went wide and her cheeks flushed. "That's not what I meant. What I mean is the man behind the Twitter craziness," she corrected quickly. "The public needs to know that you are willing to put yourself out there to find the one."

I scanned the sheet again. "Are you sure this is our best plan of action? I'm not exactly the type of man to do live video chats or do any type of counseling. Shit just seems unnecessary to me. I don't need it."

She shook her head. "I disagree with you, Mr. Madden. I told you that my plan was unconventional, but I also know that everything you've done in the past hasn't worked. It's time for you to do something drastic and this isn't something that any of your Twitter followers or the media would expect, yet, I guarantee thousands will tune in to witness your journey to find love."

Journey to find love? I sighed. She said it as if it were as easy as picking which tie I would wear every morning. Despite my misgivings about this plan, I let the idea fester in my mind a little. I didn't want to admit it, but I couldn't deny what she'd presented as being true. "Who is the matchmaker anyway?"

"Dr. Ruth Parker who has over forty years of experience. Her agency is in Boston, but she's often in New York."

"I've heard of her."

"She's close friends with Dr. Walker, so together, they really want to see this process succeed."

Leaning back in the office chair, I stared at the ceiling. It was something I'd been doing since I was a kid whenever I was too overwhelmed. "A matchmaker. A love doctor. And a live series of social media videos. It's like some twisted ass ABC dating show and I'm at the center of it all. Even if you're right, I hate this plan."

I hadn't even heard her stand from her seat until she was leaning over me, her beautiful curls falling against her face, and saying, "You forgot to mention an image consultant who is determined to help you grow from this and a team of employees who have your best interests at heart. We don't expect this to be like the shows where in the end, you propose and marry soon after. However, we do expect for you to find someone you like and could possibly build a future with. The public needs to see you try. Just think of this as a way of gaining back your life and demanding that Twitter give you back what it took."

There were a lot of emotions flooding through my mind in this moment, including the fact that I was nervous as hell to be on camera. I was an artist so I preferred to be behind the scenes. I also didn't believe in talking to a counselor about love and relationships, especially when thousands of people may possibly be watching.

But as I looked up at her and stared into those bright and hopeful eyes, I knew I would agree to this crazy ass plan before we left the conference room. Dating five women was nothing. Hell, I'd dated more than that in a month before. Problem was, my brother's dumb ass voice was in the back of my mind reminding me that the type of woman I thought I would marry—at least as far as looks go—was standing right above me. We didn't know much about each other and we had to keep things strictly business, but business was the last thing on my mind whenever I was around her and *that* posed as a real problem.

EIGHT

Malakai

"Let me get this straight. You let that beautiful brown pixie talk you into working with a matchmaker to find five women who you will date your sorry ass and have your dates be recorded for all of Twitterland and the media to watch?"

I released the basketball and shot another two-pointer, trying to ignore Crayson's teasing. "Can we just forget about it and finish this one-on-one game? I have to meet with the matchmaker and counselor in a couple hours."

Crayson continued talking as if he hadn't heard me. "And to top it all off, you also have to meet with a love doctor to discuss your dates and your *feelings*."

I forcefully tossed the ball at him since he wouldn't shut up about my situation. "Did you come out here to play ball or talk shit?"

"Bruh, you know me." He shot the ball and landed two

points as well. "Talking shit is in my DNA. Must have gotten it from Dad's side."

I huffed. "Nah, bruh. That shit is all you. Your mouth is the reason some of Dad's family stopped inviting us to the family reunions. You don't know when to shut up."

Crayson outstretched his arms. "Hey, it's not my fault that no one knew Uncle Felix was messing around with Auntie Ruthie's best friend and her best friend's daughter. I mean damn, how the hell did he keep that shit straight?"

I snorted and landed a three-pointer. "I'm not sure that was common knowledge, and keep in mind that the reunion before that one, you'd already announced to some of the fellas that cousin Ed was cheating on his wife with cousin Perry's wife."

"Bruh, I bet Auntie Ruthie knew Uncle Felix was a pimp when they met. She didn't seem that damn surprised when I accidentally slipped up. And cousin Perry couldn't have been that mad at cousin Ed because he was sleeping with Perry's wife. I bet you after I revealed that shit, they had some twisted foursome."

I stopped dribbling and shook my head. "Your mind is sick and twisted."

"I'm not twisted. Uncle Felix and cousins Ed and Perry are the twisted ones." Crayson scrunched his eyebrows together. "How are we related to Uncle Felix and Auntie Ruthie anyway? It's Dad's aunt and uncle, right? Making them our great aunt and uncle. Or, are they just family friends who we call aunt and uncle because they've been around so long?"

"I don't know, man," I said with a laugh. "Besides, twisted or not, you know folks don't like airing out their dirty laundry in front of an audience. Especially folks down south."

Crayson smiled slyly. "Unless you're my big brother because you, my dude, are gonna have to air out all of your dirty laundry live on social media. The internet never forgets."

"Tell me about it," I mumbled under my breath. If the internet was forgiving, I wouldn't be in this mess in the first place. "Honestly, although the gallery is doing good and I'm still getting requests for custom artwork, my elite clientele took a bit of a hit when those tweets and pics leaked on Twitter. For some folks, it's all about your associations or how you're perceived to the outside world, so I really need this live dating plan to work."

I passed Crayson the ball and enjoyed the few minutes of silence we had until he said, "You can say her name, you know? It may hurt, but you should say it."

I shrugged and pretended not to know what he was talking about.

"I'm serious," he continued, holding the ball hostage. "I know you, Malakai, and I've been there for all of the shit you've gone through. Of all my brothers, we understand each other the most, so I would be doing you a disservice if I didn't point out the fact that you don't have to do this live dating thing if you don't want to. You don't have to prove shit to anyone, especially a bunch of strangers and online lurkers who spend all day living through others."

I smiled, appreciating Crayson's support. For all of his faults, Crayson made up for it in heart even though he'd never let the world see it. I was close to all of my brothers, but Crayson was the only one who'd been around for some of the ups and downs I'd had in life. I loved him for it, even if he was a pain in the ass.

"So, I have another question," Crayson said, finally

getting back to the basketball game. "Are you attracted to your image consultant?"

I froze, his question catching me off guard. "Why the hell would you ask that?"

"What do you mean why the hell would I ask that? It was pretty damn obvious to everyone who was in that interview that you were attracted to her. I was just wondering if you decided what you were going to do about that attraction."

I shrugged. "Nothing. I'm not going to do anything about it."

Crayson shot a three-pointer and landed the shot. "But you do admit that you're attracted to her?"

I didn't answer right away and kept playing ball. After missing my next two shots, I finally replied, "I'm attracted to her."

Crayson smirked. "Thought so."

"And I may or may not have also told her that I want to keep things strictly professional since I've gone through so much craziness with previous consultants."

"Why the fuck did you tell her that?" Crayson yelled, waving his hands in front of him. "Think about how fucked up it's going to look to her when you go back on your word and start giving her your fuck me eyes."

"Fuck me eyes? Where the hell do you come up with this shit?"

"Bruh, we're Madden men. We all have fuck me eyes," he said matter-of-factly.

"It's a moot point anyway, because nothing is going to happen between Ms. Nightingale and I."

Crayson slapped me on the back. "Ms. Nightingale? Dude, who the hell are you kidding? You may have been denying yourself the pleasure of a hot-blooded woman for a year, but something tells me that your dry spell will be over soon since you're going to be dating five women." He shot the ball and landed the winning shot. "I'm just curious to see if it will be one of those women who pop your yearlong cherry, or if it will be the woman responsible for making the dates happen."

As much as I hated to admit that Crayson made sense about anything, he was right. Despite what was right and what was wrong, I had the same underlying question. Problem was, I wasn't sure how long it would take for me to figure out the answer.

Avery

WHERE IN THE *world is he?* I glanced at my phone for the fifth time in the past couple minutes, hoping that Malakai would arrive soon. Dr. Walker and Dr. Parker had arrived early and were already in the conference room.

"He'll be here in time," Ms. Woodstock said, interrupting her sixth-time glancing at her phone. "He still has five minutes before the meeting was scheduled to begin."

"I know he still has time. I'm just anxious, that's all." Despite how confident I'd seemed when I'd presented my plan a couple days ago, inside, tiny baby elephants had been doing backflips in my stomach.

There were so many things that could happen and cause this plan to fail. For starters, Malakai could decide not to be as open about his dates and relationship status during the live counseling sessions as he'd agreed to be. Second, live videos can be tricky, so he could reveal more than what they'd originally discussed.

Third, the matchmaker could fail to find him a person who he really connects with despite her success rate. And fourth ... *You know what the fourth thing is. Just say it!* Even if I didn't want to admit it to myself, the fourth and only reason that truly affected me was the fact that he might find the woman he wants to marry during this process.

True, I wanted him to find love and my job was to help him improve his image so that he could go about doing so. However, I couldn't deny that a part of me wished I could be the woman he falls for. Mixing business and pleasure was wrong, especially in this case. But it didn't stop me from daydreaming about his brown-cinnamon spice complexion and luscious lips. Or wondering how deep his hazel gaze got when he was all hot and bothered. Sometimes, my tongue grew heavy as I thought about the places I'd love to lick and explore along his body. Or I'd be in meetings and have to stop myself from staring too long at his crotch area. I didn't have an obsession with staring at dick or anything, but his imprint through his pants was hard not to look at. He walked as if it were big as hell, and judging by that online photo, he was packing some long and thick heat. Something told me his dick could put me in a wheelchair if I wasn't careful. But if I had to lose all function in my legs ... "What a way to go."

"What is that, dear?" Ms. Woodstock asked.

I shook my head from its lustful fog. "Uh, nothing. I was just thinking about a movie I saw."

"Um, hmm." She glanced at me above the rim of her

glasses. "Must have been some movie based off the way you were moaning."

Moaning? Instead of mentally slapping my forehead with my hand, I went ahead and did the movement. On cue, the object of my outburst came strolling past the elevators.

He was sporting a blue-grey suit and walked with a sort of confidence that would make some men wish they could be that smooth. My eyes lifted to meet his and the wink and smile he flashed at me had me inwardly fainting to the floor. I remember my grandma once telling me that my grandfather used to walk into a room and instantly, her lips began to quiver at the sexy sight of him. "He was so irresistible, there wasn't a part of me that wasn't wet," she'd said.

At the time, I shuddered at the visual she'd placed in my head, and although she went on to explain that all she meant was that she was nervous and sweating all over, the damage had already been done. I couldn't listen to the rest of the story after that.

It may have taken me years to appreciate Grams' sentiment, but I finally knew what it meant to have your lips quiver at the sight of a man. *Don't stare at him too long, Nightingale. Otherwise, you'll never make it through this meeting.* My hand flew up to my bottom lip just in case my lips didn't listen to my warning.

"Are you ready?" I asked as he approached.

"As ready as I'll ever be."

"Great, because Dr. Walker and Dr. Parker are already here."

He took a deep breath. "Let's get this over with."

I motioned for him to go ahead so I could compose myself. I hadn't even known Ms. Woodstock had been watching my every move until I heard her say, "Dear, try not to drool during the meeting."

My eyes flew to hers. "Was it that obvious?"

"Only because I was paying attention," she replied. "Besides, he stares at you just as hard, so don't sweat it."

My girly parts did a somersault. I tried my best to keep the hopefulness out my voice when I said, "He does?"

Her eyes grew concerned. "Yes, he does, but he needs you and not in the dating kind of way. All of us are impressed by what you've done so far and we think you may just be the one to really turn around his image. He needs you more as his consultant than his lover."

Well, damn. While I wanted to ask her why I couldn't be both, I settled for, "I understand and I agree. I want what's best for him and I plan on doing a great job."

"Glad to hear it." She reached over and lightly squeezed my hand before reminding me that the meeting was starting.

When I reached the conference room, introductions were already being made. I waited a few seconds before saying, "Let's get started."

While Dr. Walker and Dr. Parker gave me hopeful smiles, Malakai's forced smile seemed that of someone doped up on Novocain after leaving the dentist's office.

"Mr. Madden and I would like to thank you both for being here," I stated, focusing on the task at hand and diving into my speech. "As you both know, our goal is to find Mr. Madden the woman of his dreams while also changing his image in the public eye. However, I think to get to the solution to the problem, we must start at the roots."

"I couldn't agree more." Dr. Walker turned his attention to Malakai. "Mr. Madden, I know you aren't completely on board with having live counseling sessions, but I want to assure you that at the end of the day, I want you to feel comfortable. I've been with my wife for nearly fifty years and I have over thirty years of experience in relationship and marriage counseling. What I've found is that there is something extremely vulnerable and uninhibited by opening up in front of an audience whether that be in person or online."

Malakai clenched his jaw. I wasn't sure the others noticed it, but I did. "I've researched your methods, Dr. Walker, and although it's clear that you're great at what you do, I find little comfort in baring my soul in front of a bunch of strangers."

"That's understandable," Dr. Walker said. "I can't promise you that some of the discussions won't be more private than you'd like, but I think after a few sessions you'll find it therapeutic."

Malakai didn't look convinced, but I figured it would take more than this meeting to truly convince him. He had to experience the process for himself. He had to get familiar with sharing more about himself to the public.

"How will you find the women I'm supposed to date?" he asked.

"That's where I come in," Dr. Parker said. "Within the next couple days, you and I will sit down and talk about what you're looking for in a relationship. I will do my best to match you with five women who fit what you're looking for." Dr. Parker linked her hands together. "And if I'm being honest, Mr. Madden, I must tell you that I've already received several calls from women who asked if you were one of my clients."

He quirked an eyebrow. "You can't be serious. We haven't even shared news yet about me dating."

"It doesn't matter." Dr. Parker shook her head. "As soon as you posted a tweet confirming that you were indeed trying to find the woman you would marry, my inbox was flooded with emails and the phones wouldn't stop ringing. You are quite sought after, Mr. Madden, which is why I can't wait to pair you with some amazing women."

"From what Ms. Nightingale has told me," Malakai began, "it's not expected that I marry someone at the end of this like those reality television shows, correct?"

"Absolutely not," Dr. Parker answered. "We don't expect you to propose after this process, but I wouldn't be one of the top experts in my field if I didn't try and pair with you five women who could be potential mates for life."

"We've done some research on you," Dr. Walker interjected. "You have a lot of good to offer in a relationship, but as you well know, because of everything that happened on Twitter, most of the public only sees you as a sex symbol and the media is all too happy to portray you that way. Our goal is to wipe that image clean. We don't need or want to change you. We just want the public to get a taste of the real Malakai Madden."

"The process will last for a few weeks," I said, chiming in. "At certain times throughout the process, you'll decide which women you want to continue dating, eliminating the one you have the least connection with. You can choose to stop dating more than one or maybe none for the first couple of weeks. All I ask is that the last week, you have your choice narrowed down to no more than two women."

He squinted his eyes. "Hmm, sounds a lot like those reality shows I warned you I didn't want to be like." His eyes were laughing, but I knew it was a real concern of his.

"It's not," I said quickly. "Well, sort of, but not really."

"Not really?" His smile was full-fledged now. "Should I hand out roses after every elimination?"

I smiled back at him as I shook my head. "There isn't going to be any live eliminations. You will simply decide who you no longer want to date. And the only roses you will hand out are ones you choose to buy for any of your dates. The women we choose to do this process with will be aware of the situation."

"Precisely," Dr. Walker agreed. "During your sessions with me, we will show highlights from your dates and then dive into our chat."

"The first live session with Dr. Walker will kick off in a few days," I added. "It's a chance for the public to get to know you and for us to introduce this new venture on your journey to love."

He grinned at me, the curve of his lips doing crazy things to my insides. "My journey to love? Is that what we're calling it?"

I shrugged off the unwanted butterflies, along with his comment. "I just made it up, but we can come up with a better name."

Dr. Parker clasped her hands together. "I have a team of people who could help us create something catchy. I've asked that Dr. Walker assist me in the matching process. We've worked together before and we both want you to ultimately find what you are looking for. All we ask is that you let us help you any way we can for this part of your journey."

The sincerity in their voices seemed to coax away some of the worry lines in Malakai's forehead. As Dr. Walker and Dr. Parker continued to go over the details of the process that we'd previously discussed, I took a moment to observe Malakai. Sometimes he seemed confident about the plan, while at other times, he appeared unsure.

That makes two of us. As his image consultant, I had to maintain my optimism and ensure that I came across confident in my plan so that he felt comfortable as well.

Inwardly, I was a nervous wreck, but there was one thing I knew for sure ... Dr. Walker and Dr. Parker were right. Malakai Madden was an extremely good catch and it was about damn time the rest of the world got to know the side of him that he often kept hidden.

NINE

Malakai

There were a few times in my life when I found myself in bullshit that I couldn't get out of. Like now. The Twitter bullshit had caused me to have to deal with public image bullshit that had now morphed into live video bullshit that I didn't want to do.

Don't get me wrong, I understood the benefit of working with Dr. Walker and Dr. Parker, but damn, I wished I didn't have to get on camera to get back my private life that Twitter stole. To top things off, Avery was running late and would probably arrive toward the end of the segment. As much as I hated to need anybody, I wanted her there and wished I could soak in her calmness and warmth before we started the first live video.

One would think that by now, I could identify that SOB named *bullshit* a mile away, especially given my intimate acquaintance with him. No, scratch that ... bullshit was definitely a woman since my love for women was what got me into this mess in the first place.

The first time was back in grammar school when my family lived in Little Rock before moving to Cranberry Heights. I let some idiots talk me into breaking into our school to log into the main school computer and change our grades.

It was stupid and the crazy thing is, I didn't even need my grades changed. I had already been getting A's and B's. When the security guard found us, everyone scattered and I was the lucky bastard who ran into the desk chair and fell, taking the computer with me. Not one of those guys stopped to help me up. The school didn't play with break-ins and decided to use me as an example. Instead of getting suspended like I'd hoped, or working off paying the fee for the computer I'd broken, the new principal expelled me, no questions asked. My parents had been pissed, but not as much as I had been at myself.

Switching schools in the middle of the year hadn't been as bad as I'd thought, and by the time we moved to Cranberry Heights, it was almost time for me to start high school. High school brought an entirely new set of problems. I'd gone from this awkward, gangly pre-teen to a tall, athletic teenager with more curly hair than I knew what to do with. I had a lot of guy friends on the surface, but for the most part, there were only a handful of men who truly knew me. It took a while for me to be accepted in high school, but I quickly got the hang of it and learned how to be myself.

Regardless of the clarity I eventually got in high school, I still had to deal with certain bullshit. Some of the guys despised me because I seemed to come in and automatically gain popularity status, while some of the girls didn't care to want to know me, but rather, only wanted to fuck me.

After high school, bullshit came to grace my life with her presence a few more times, and then bam, I'm hit with my current predicament.

"We're starting in two minutes," said Steve, Dr. Walker's cameraman.

I nodded my head and adjusted my bowtie, unsure of what to expect and trying to remember that I had to just be myself.

It had been three days since Dr. Parker and Dr. Walker met with Avery and I to go over the details of the live sessions. Today, we were all gathered at Dr. Walker's place of business and were introducing a series of live videos that were unfortunately titled "Malakai Madden's Journey to Love". It wasn't that I hated the title, but damn, it really did make me feel like I was in one of those wacky reality love shows.

"Are you ready?" Dr. Walker asked.

"I will be."

Dr. Parker was also seated with us for the introduction. Although I'd already met with her a couple days ago to discuss what I wanted in the women I dated, she wanted to ask me a few questions live to help with the segment.

As I saw Tyler talking with Ben, the director, I was glad that I'd asked him to come along for the session. I didn't care about all of the technical details, but Tyler loved that shit, and despite the fact that Dr. Walker and Dr. Parker seemed trustworthy, I needed someone in that room who was looking out for me.

When Ben gave us the countdown, I pushed aside my nerves and focused on the task at hand—giving America a taste of Malakai Madden.

"Ladies and gentlemen," Dr. Walker said. "Today, I am excited to announce a very special guest who will be doing a series of live counseling sessions with me, Dr. William Walker, and a dear friend, matchmaker extraordinaire, Dr. Ruth Parker." He motioned his hand in my direction. "Mr. Malakai Madden, I am so honored to have the pleasure to work with you. How about you remind the people who you are and we'll tell them a little about this live video series."

"Sure, thank you for having me, Dr. Walker." Adjusting myself in my seat, I briefly glanced at the screen to the left of where we were recording that had displayed the number of views and tweets coming through. "As some of the viewers may know, a year ago, some extremely private information was leaked about me and as a result, I opened up about the fact that I was anxious to be in a serious and committed relationship that would hopefully result in finding my wife.

"I was overwhelmed by the amount of feedback I received, and after careful consideration, I've decided to partner with Parker Matchmaking in hopes of finding the perfect woman for me."

Dr. Walker smiled. "That's very exciting to hear. I'm sure folks can't wait to follow along on your journey."

"Thank you, Dr. Walker. I sure hope so."

"And that's not all," Dr. Walker said enthusiastically. "In addition to partnering with Parker Matchmaking, I will also be doing counseling sessions with Mr. Madden along the way to peel back his layers and discuss his dates in an intimate setting."

Intimate setting? I highly doubted laying out my feelings in front of everyone in Twitterland was intimate. More like the complete opposite. "Yes, we will. And we have a great name for it." Just as I was explaining, Avery walked into the office. Her eyes scanned the few people in the room before landing on me and blessing me with a beautiful smile.

Per usual, she looked breathtaking. Today, she was sporting a green dress that was tight at the top, but flared out at the waist. Immediately, my eyes went to her sweet, dark honey legs. Legs that I knew would feel amazing wrapped around me.

She shook her hands and only then did I notice the umbrella and the fact that her hair looked slightly damp. Despite the rain she'd clearly been caught in, her curls still looked full and bounced as she made her way to a corner of the room where Tyler was standing. When she reached up to her hair to fluff it out, I noticed she was wearing her feather ring again, only this time, she was wearing matching feather earrings.

"Mr. Madden?"

My head swung back to Dr. Walker. "I'm sorry, what was the question?"

He chuckled and Dr. Parker stifled a laugh. "I didn't ask a question. You were speaking, but I guess you needed a few moments to gather your thoughts. You were just about to share the name of this video series."

"Right." I shifted in my chair. "The name of the video series will be 'Malakai Madden's Journey to Love'. The name was suggested by a friend, but it's slowly growing on me."

I smiled as I stole a quick glance in Avery's direction before turning my attention back to Dr. Walker.

"I think 'Malakai Madden's Journey to Love' fits precisely what you're about to embark upon," Dr. Walker said. "Now, Dr. Parker, I understand that you've already met with Mr. Madden regarding his expectations for your partnership. Is that correct?"

"It is, Dr. Walker," she replied with a smile. "We had the pleasure of speaking earlier this week, and I must say, it was refreshing to talk to a man who not only knows exactly what he wants in a woman, but is confident in what he brings to the table as well." Dr. Parker turned to me. "Mr. Madden, can you share with us a few qualities and characteristics that you look for in a potential partner?"

Okay, here's when the real work begins. The first few minutes were just the warm-up. Now, it was time for me to dive in.

I took a deep breath, steadying my voice as I answered, "I suppose what I want in a potential partner is simple and what most people want. I'm looking for my best friend. A woman who I can talk about my day with and bounce ideas off. I'm looking for a woman who isn't afraid to speak her mind, and while independent, also works great as a team because ultimately, she and I will be a team.

"I'm looking for a woman who can laugh when times get hard and overcome obstacles when faced with adversity. I need a woman who has heart and soul. One who will support me no matter what. And in return, I promise to be her main support system in any way she needs me. For a relationship to work, each person must give and take equally. Granted, there will be times when one person needs to give a little more to be there for the other person, but I welcome those times. I want to cater to my woman. Rub her feet after a long day. Cook her favorite food when she needs to be cheered up."

As if they had a mind of their own, my eyes found Avery's. "I'm looking for a woman with a kind and generous heart who can see past the layers that I've placed over my heart and get to know the real Malakai Madden. Not the man the media portrays him to be, but rather, the man who would give anything to find the woman he's meant to share the rest of his life with and love her with all that I am."

Even from a short distance, I could see her breath catch and her mouth slightly part. If she felt like I was talking to her, it was because I was. I wasn't trying to make her the central point of my discussion, but there I was, dragging my eyes to hers any chance I got and not giving a damn that thousands of people online were probably wondering what the hell I was staring at.

"Sounds like some woman," Dr. Walker said, breaking my trance.

Leaning over, Dr. Parker gently touched my hand. "Those are wonderful qualities and characteristics, Mr. Madden, and I know she's out there waiting for you."

"I agree," Dr. Walker added. "So tell me this. When did you figure out you were ready to find the person you want to spend the rest of your life with?"

His question should have been easy to answer because I'd asked myself the same thing for over a year. After thinking about it for so long, I knew the answer. But I wasn't ready to be that honest to the public just yet. So instead, I settled on saying, "When I turned thirty-four over a year and a half ago, I had to take a hard look at my life and figure out where I wanted to be in the next couple of years. I've always been a man with a plan, yet every time I thought about what I wanted to accomplish, I realized that every accomplishment would seem mediocre if I didn't have a woman to share my life with. I knew I was ready to not just experience the forever kind of love, but to immerse myself in it ... in one woman." Not exactly the best answer, but one that would have to do.

Dr. Walker seemed to be satisfied with my answer. "Immersed in love ... I like it."

The rest of the session flowed and I loosened up even more as time went on. After the session ended, I was told several times that I'm a natural on camera, which was funny considering I didn't care for the spotlight shit one bit.

Everyone seemed even more impressed by the fact that close to one hundred thousand people had tuned into the session. I was only partially listening to them since it always seemed that I could only halfway pay attention whenever Avery was in the room.

She fidgeted with her fingers, and her laugh when someone made a joke about some of the tweets about the session seemed fake to me. I'd heard her real laugh. It was soft, like a fluffy pillow laying on a smooth velvet bedspread. This one wasn't bad. It just wasn't Avery.

I could also tell that she appeared to be ignoring me. When we were recording, our eyes met, yet now, she wouldn't even look my way. Didn't someone tell her that I was the type of dude that didn't mind the chase when it was something I wanted? Hell, I wouldn't be surprised if the others in the room could feel the sexual tension flowing between our bodies.

I wasn't an idiot. I was the one who'd told Avery that we couldn't date based off what I'd gone through with previous image consultants. I appreciated her agreeance, but didn't she realize as the creator of the rule I could just as easily throw that shit out the window? I would never do anything to make her uncomfortable, but something told me that I needed to figure out more about Avery Nightingale.

TEN

Avery

Gimmie. Gimmie. Gimmie. I grabbed the tequila shot from Jordyn's hand before she had a chance to place it on the table.

"Whoa, friend! You know you're a lightweight. Take it easy."

"She can't take it easy," Tyler said, shaking his head. "Boss man said he may stop by the bar and Avery is losing her shit over that possibility."

Serenity accepted the drink she'd ordered from Jordyn. "Okay, I wasn't at the Twitter live session earlier and I haven't seen it yet, so can one of you clue me in on what happened?"

I opened my mouth to speak, but my tongue was still stinging from the liquor. Tyler was all too happy to tell the ladies for me. "Oh yes, girl. But it's better that we show you." He pulled his phone out of his pocket and went to the video, scrolling the bar until he got to the part where Malakai was talking about what he wants in a woman.

"Did you memorize exactly where that part was?" I whispered to Tyler.

"Down to the minute."

I shook my head before tuning into the video. Tyler had stopped at the part where he was still speaking directly to Dr. Walker and Dr. Parker. As it got closer to the part where Malakai turned toward my way, I was sure my face looked like I'd just gotten out of a hot shower.

He spoke with ease and I noticed a comfortability in his demeanor that I hadn't recognized before since I'd been too busy staring back at him in disbelief that he was holding my gaze while he talked.

Here it was. That last line that really did me in. "... the man who would give anything to find the woman he's meant to share the rest of his life with and love her with all that I am."

Even now, my heart was pounding in my chest at his words. I wasn't sure there was any woman who could ignore that deep hazel gaze when it was pierced to hers.

"Wow," Serenity said breathlessly.

"I'm taking a break," Jordyn yelled toward one of her bartenders before taking a seat in the empty chair next to me.

Tyler smacked his lips together. "Told you ladies that you needed to hear it. And in case you didn't catch it since Avery wasn't in the video, he was looking directly at her when he was saying that last part."

"I thought so." Jordyn's eyes widened in recognition. "But didn't you say that Malakai had asked that you keep your relationship strictly business as you cleaned up his image?"

I nodded my head. "Yes, that's exactly what he asked."

"I think he's into you." Serenity took a sip of her drink. "Whenever you both are in the same room together, he's secretly giving you those looks."

I scrunched my eyebrows together. "What do you mean? How exactly does he look at me?"

Serenity lifted her eyes to the ceiling as if she were thinking hard about the question. "Like he's stuck on a deserted island and instead of water, all he needs to quench his thirst is you."

"Damn," Jordyn muttered. "Can't remember the last time a man looked at me like that."

I shook my head. "Even if he did look at me like that, it can't happen. I'm literally spearheading his journey to find a woman he can spend the rest of his life with, and last time I checked, close to one hundred thousand people tuned in for the kickoff."

"News flash, honey," Tyler said, snapping his fingers. "M&M may have already found that woman. I know you didn't plan on it, but I think you should be dating him."

I reached for the water that Jordyn had brought to the table. "Tyler, you and Serenity know better than most that the last thing Malakai needs is another image consultant losing focus on bettering his image and wanting nothing more than to get in his pants or use him for their own personal gain."

Serenity shook her head. "You're nothing like the others. And you can't help it if you have sexual chemistry. Maybe it's worth a try to at least feel him out and see if he's feeling the same way."

I let out a groan that was loud enough to get the attention from folks at the table next to us. I knew what my friends saw. Hell, I felt it every time I looked at

Malakai. *Girl, please. You felt that shit before you even met the man.*

For every reason I could find to validate my attraction to him, I could find ten more reasons why I shouldn't even go there. I voiced just that when I said, "It can't happen. I take my job seriously and Malakai Madden is the biggest client I've ever had independently. I can't fuck this up."

"You won't." Tyler looked at her sympathetically. "Just give it a shot. Worst case scenario, you both realize you're better as business associates. Best case scenario, you start to date, have some amazing sex, and realize that the cat and mouse game wasn't necessary. A talk can't hurt, right?"

"Yeah, it can." I threw my hands up in exaggeration. Didn't they get it? Had they followed all of the info released on Twitter like I had? Once I went down that rabbit hole, there was no way I was going to come out of it the same. They didn't know the entire story. Maybe if they did, they wouldn't even be entertaining this.

"Sorry if I seem adamant about this, but it can't happen," I said aloud. *Just tell them why. You're amongst friends.* "Guys, if I tell you this, it stays between us, right?"

"Of course," Serenity said.

Jordyn smiled. "Girl, you already know the answer."

"Spill the tea." Tyler perked up in his chair. "You know we got you."

Taking a deep breath, I said the words as quickly as I could. "ThereasonIcan'tgotherewithMalakaiisbecauseI'veneverhadanorgasmbeforeandI'mworriedonenightwithhimwouldcompletelywreckmeforothermen."

Serenity and Jordyn both gave me confused looks while Tyler all but shrieked as his hand flew to his mouth.

"You understood that?" Serenity asked him.

"Yes," he said slowly, still in shock. "And if I heard

correctly, our girl here just dropped some thick truth serum by admitting that she's never had an orgasm before."

Now it was Serenity and Jordyn's time to gasp in shock. *Fucking great.* As if I didn't think that I was enough of an anomaly and probably the only woman in her thirties to never have an orgasm, the expressions on their faces weren't helping matters.

"I've had them before of my own doing, but not during sex or anything oral." *Shit, that sounds sad.* I hated feeling like I was on display. "Look, it's not as bad as it sounds."

"The hell it is." Tyler shook his head. "That's a big deal and something that anyone who is sexually active should have the pleasure of feeling."

"You're right." I dropped my head to the table. "I'm a freak."

"Not a freak." Reaching over the table, Serenity began to rub my arm. "It may be a little surprising, but it's not that unusual. There are plenty of women who haven't had orgasms before."

"So let me get this straight ..." Jordyn's brow furrowed. "You've never had an orgasm before and now, you're the image consultant for the man who the media has deemed Mr. Make You Moan since he delivers multiple orgasms?"

I cringed at her words. "Unfortunately, yes. That's right."

"I wasn't thinking unfortunate." Jordyn leaned closer so that her voice wouldn't carry. "I was thinking more like *jackpot.* I was trying to stay neutral and not pressure you, but I agree with Tyler and Serenity. You need to have that conversation with Malakai and tell him what's up."

"What am I supposed to say?" I asked. "Just pull him aside one day and say 'Malakai, you may not know this, but I've fantasized about us together more times than I can count. Can you do me a huge favor and pop my orgasm cherry? I'd be forever grateful for your act of service'."

Tyler frowned. "Maybe not like that."

"Yeah, definitely not like that," Serenity added.

Jordyn shook her head. "Friend, we need to work on your macking skills."

"I shouldn't have told you guys." My shoulders slumped a little. "It's bad enough I spend half ... if not all of my meetings with that man daydreaming about him naked. There is no way in hell I could build up the nerve to actually ask him to give me an orgasm."

The loud clearing of a voice caused each of us at the table to jump at the sound. Goosebumps on my arm. Masculine scent lingering in the air. Conversation at the table ceasing immediately. I slowly lifted my head from the spot on the table that briefly served as my refuge, but I knew who it was before my eyes even locked on that penetrating hazel gaze. *Shit. Shit. Shit. Shit. Shit.* Clearly, none of us had heard Malakai arrive at the table and my heart started doing somersaults at the thought that he'd overheard what we'd been talking about.

"Glad I was able to catch you all." He may have been talking to everyone at the table, but his eyes were solely on me. After pulling up a stool from an empty table, he sat at the edge. When his left knee brushed against mine, I sucked in my breath.

"What did I miss?" Once again, he was looking at me. *Damn.* It didn't take a genius to figure out that the smirk on his lips meant that he'd overheard enough of the conversation.

As much as I wished my voice sounded convincing, I knew it didn't when my, "Nothing," was met with a, "Really?" I didn't want to give him the satisfaction of rolling my eyes. Especially when he seemed to anticipate that I'd never tell him the truth.

"Do you really want to know what we were talking about?" *Avery, what the hell are you doing? If he says yes, what will you say?*

His lips curled into a wide smile. "Sure do."

Crap. I hadn't jumped off the cliff yet, but I was damn sure steps away from falling over the edge. I chanced a quick glance at my friends, hoping that someone would throw me a Save-A-Bitch rope and pull me to safety. Instead of any help with the situation, Jordyn sat with a sly smile on her face, Serenity was sporting a look of interested sincerity, and Tyler had his hands clasped together anxiously, his eyes bouncing between Malakai and me.

It's all on you, Nightingale. My eyes made their way back to Malakai, his bearded face and juicy lips causing me to mask a moan that was sure to make the situation more awkward.

Mustering up all the courage I could, I stared at him straight in the eyes and said, "You, Mr. Madden. We were talking about you, me, and the fact that ..." My voice trailed off as I got to the part that I really didn't want to say out loud. What was I thinking? Regardless of what my friends thought, saying anything to him would be a huge mistake. A terrible mistake. A mistake that I couldn't take back once I said the words.

"What fact would that be?" he asked, his voice deeper than how he'd previously sounded. I noticed the way he clenched and unclenched his jaw as seconds ticked past without me saying anything else.

"Uh." I fidgeted with the straw in my water. "I mean. What I was going to say was. Um—"

"Hey," a loud voice called as he approached, interrupting me. "What's up, people?"

The last of the breath that I'd been holding released as Crayson walked up to our table.

Serenity rolled her eyes. "You have terrible timing."

"The worst," Tyler added.

"The best." I scooted over so that he could pull up a stool and sit between Malakai and me. I couldn't even look his way for fear that those hazel eyes would bore into my soul until I told him the rest of my secret. Well, my not-so-secret-anymore secret.

"Sorry I'm late," Crayson said. "Malakai didn't tell me y'all were meeting here until an hour ago." As if he noticed Jordyn for the first time, Crayson stopped speaking. "Well, hello there, beautiful. I don't believe we've had the pleasure of meeting." He extended his hand to Jordyn, but instead of taking it, she just stared at him.

"I'm going to get back to work," she stated, still ignoring Crayson's hand. "Avery, call me later."

I nodded my head as Crayson watched Jordyn walk away. "Damn, she's got an ass on her."

Serenity slapped his arm. "And you wonder why she wouldn't give you the time of day. Do you ever think about how you talk to women?"

"Don't take it seriously," Tyler said. "She treated me the same way before she realized she wasn't my type."

Crayson nodded, directing his attention to Malakai. "I saw your video on Twitter, but I wanted to hear from you how it went."

It was only then that I finally glanced Malakai's way. However, instead of looking at his brother like I expected, he was staring at me. I swallowed the lump in my throat knowing that I couldn't sit there any longer with him so close.

"I better go." I stood from the table. "Crayson, you should try one of Jordyn's dessert drinks. They are delicious." I turned to the others at the table, making sure I focused my attention on Tyler and Serenity. "And I guess I will see you guys tomorrow at work. It's been fun." And by fun, I meant I'd rather be getting my vagina waxed by a heavy-handed woman right now than be here any longer.

"I'll walk you out," Malakai said, catching me off guard.

I was shaking my head before he even got out the thought. "That's not necessary. I actually live just above the bar."

He glanced at the side door that led to the stairs. "Then I'll walk you up."

Before I could oppose, he was already walking toward that direction. My eyes widened in panic as I mouthed to Tyler or Serenity to help me.

"Nope." Tyler nodded his head.

Serenity gave a sympathetic smile. "Sorry, girlfriend."

Crayson looked from them, to me, to his retreating brother. "What the hell did I miss?"

Instead of staying behind to see if they filled him in, I followed the direction that Malakai had gone. *What in the world am I going to do?* Malakai Madden wasn't the type of man to believe a bullshit answer and I wasn't clever enough to come up with a sufficient excuse if he'd overheard any part of the conversation.

When he reached the side door, he held it open for me to walk past him. I held my breath so that I wouldn't breathe in any more of his enticing scent than I already was, but it was no use once we began climbing the stairs. The narrow stairway seemed even smaller than normal, and by the time we reached my door, I was consumed with all thoughts Malakai and hadn't come up with an alternative answer to give him to his lingering question.

"Well, here I am," I said, my back toward him. There was no way I was turning around. No way was I going to gaze into those breathtaking eyes. The lust floating in the air around us was suffocating me more than I'd ever admit to myself.

He took a step closer, my backside extremely close to the front of him if the heat radiating between us was any indicator. On one hand, my common sense—who I'd affectionately named Halo—was telling me that letting him get this close was a bad idea and warning me to quickly let myself into my apartment and send him on his way. Yet, that she-devil on my shoulder—better known as Coco—was saying, "Yassss, bitch. Let his fine ass in."

As we stood there in silence, with my back still toward him, I could slowly see Halo being knocked off my shoulder to the ground by Coco. I was fumbling with my keys, when I heard him groan, which was the only noise he'd made since we got to my apartment. *Was that a good moan? A bad moan? A would-she-tell-me-what-the-hell-she-was-about-to-say moan?* I wasn't sure.

Outwardly, I was remaining calm. Inwardly, I was cursing out Coco for weakening my resolve when it came to this man. I finally got my keys in the lock and turned to face Malakai just as I was opening the door.

I opened my mouth to speak, but the fire reflected in his eyes made my words die on my tongue. He took a step closer, which caused me to take a step back into my apartment.

He squinted his eyes as if he were trying to gauge how I

felt about whatever the hell was about to happen. "Can I come in?" he asked.

I bit my lip, the move bringing his eyes back to my mouth. *I shouldn't let him in. He's about to be dating five women soon.* I shuffled from one foot to the other. *Girl, stop playing and let him in already. You don't have to sleep with him, but you damn sure better sample those lips.*

I shook my head. "Shut up, Coco."

He laughed. "Is that a yes?"

I stepped back from my door. "Yes, come on in."

ELEVEN

Malakai

The moment I stepped into her apartment, I took a deep breath to open my mind and give me a moment to think about what my next move would be. My mind had been thinking about the words I'd overheard her say since I'd sat down at the table in the bar.

It's bad enough I spend half ... if not all of my meetings with that man daydreaming about him naked. There is no way in hell I could build up the nerve to actually ask him to give me an orgasm.

So she wanted me to give her an orgasm and often pictured me naked? Hell, didn't she know that she didn't even have to be in the vicinity for me to picture her naked, and giving her a mind-blowing orgasm would be more my pleasure than hers?

"Do you want anything to drink?" she asked.

"Nah, I'm good." I followed her into the kitchen area,

my eyes unable to leave her ass as I watched her walk to the refrigerator to get herself a water bottle.

I did a quick survey of my surroundings, noting that Avery was exactly the type of person I thought she was. A person's living quarters always told a lot about their character. In Avery's case, her furniture was modern, but unique. Her colors were warm, yet flowed together nicely. However, it was her walls that were tastefully decorated with beautiful artwork that really got my attention. Being an artist myself, I loved a woman who could appreciate good artwork.

"Are you sure you don't want anything to drink?" she asked, placing her water bottle on the counter. "I could brew some coffee or make you some tea."

"I rarely drink coffee," I said, eliminating the space between us. "And although I love tea, the only thing I want to taste on my lips right now is you." I gave her a few seconds to back away or tell me that this wasn't what she wanted. Yet, when instead of retreating, she licked her lips and leaned her head closer, I dipped my head to hers to capture the lips that had kept me up at night ever since we'd met.

She tasted just like I thought she would—sweet, with a hint of spice. It didn't take long for my tongue to coax hers open to explore her mouth in a way I hadn't done with a woman in years.

Her hands snaked up to the top of my neck while my arms went around her waist, pulling her closer to me. Avery kissed as amazing as I knew she would, her tongue working me just as much as I was working her. When I felt her growing more eager, I cupped her ass and lifted her to the counter, immediately placing myself in between her legs as we continued to kiss without breaking our rhythm.

"Malakai," she moaned in between kisses. The sound of her saying my first name and not calling me Mr. Madden was doing crazy things to my self-control. For me, kissing had always been the best type of foreplay I could get. Call me crazy, but as much as I loved giving oral sex and receiving oral sex, nothing got me hornier than a plush pair of lips and a woman who knew how to use them.

She flicked her tongue over mine in a wave that seemed to be directly connected to the sensors in my dick. I didn't want things to get too out of hand, but if she kept up that tongue action, I was going to have to break my year-long drought.

A few licks and nips later, we broke the kiss for some much-needed oxygen. I leaned my forehead against hers as I waited for my breathing to slow down.

"Damn, Avery." I lifted my head to look her in the eyes. "If I'd known you kissed like that, I would have kissed you weeks ago."

She laughed in the familiar way that I was really beginning to get attached to. "I enjoy hearing you call me Avery and not Ms. Nightingale."

I smiled. "I damn sure rather you call me Malakai."

She reached her hand between us and said, "Deal."

I took her hand in mine, my large one enveloping her smaller one in a way that seemed to perfectly connect. She must have noticed it, too, because her eyes got even brighter. A few seconds later, a frown replaced her smile.

"What is it?" I asked, my hand gently going to her cheek. "Do you regret kissing me?"

"Yes and no," she answered, using her hand for emphasis. "I enjoyed kissing you a lot more than I should have because starting tomorrow, you go on your first two of five dates."

I dropped my hand back to the counter, but didn't step away from her. Tomorrow I had a day date and a night date. Neither of which I was really thrilled to go on. The person I wanted to go on a date with was sitting right in front of me. "I know. I thought about that earlier today when I was watching you while I was recording with Dr. Walker and Dr. Parker."

Her eyes widened. "So you were watching me on purpose?"

"Not at first," I said with a laugh. "But it seemed I couldn't keep my eyes off you, so after a while, I gave up trying." My voice sounded huskier even to my own ears.

Her eyes dropped to my lips. "No matter how great that kiss was, you have to go through with this process. At the end of the day, I was hired to change your image and in doing so, I'm obligated to remember what's important here. Plus, you said we had to keep things professional. I don't want to be like your previous image consultants."

"I understand that and I appreciate it." I pulled her closer to me, the fabric of her dress making it easier to slide her on the counter. "But in case you haven't figured it out, sometimes I fuck up and make a dumb ass comment."

She laughed again. "Are you suggesting that telling us to keep things business was the dumb ass comment?"

I nodded my head. "Hell yeah. I knew that shit was stupid before the words had left my mouth."

This time, her entire body shook when she laughed and it was so infectious, I found myself laughing along with her until her face grew serious. "I meant what I said. You have to go on these dates. Your future wife could be amongst these women."

Fuck that. I wanted to tell her that although I respected Dr. Parker, I highly doubted one of those women were the future Mrs. Malakai Madden. Avery only knew my brother, Crayson, but had she met some more members of the Madden clan, someone would have told her when a Madden man sets his sights on the one woman who holds the key to his future, he wife's her up quicker than she can figure out what's going on. Just ask my brothers, Micah and Malik. Before Lex and Mya knew it, my brothers had swept them off their feet and had them walking down the aisle.

I always followed my gut and my gut was telling me that even though there was still so much I needed to learn about Avery and so much she needed to learn about me, I was done keeping my distance. I'd always been the type of man to go after what I want and Avery Nightingale had become número uno weeks ago. However, I didn't want to scare her off and laying all of my cards on the table would definitely do all that. So I'd play by her rules, or at least pretend to play by them, until the time was right.

"I'll go on these dates because you want me to, but I won't like it." I trailed kisses along the base of her neck before I made my way back to her beautiful face. "But tonight is tonight. So these lips of yours are mine until you kick me out of your place."

My lips were on hers so fast, her laugh never escaped her lips.

Avery

"AVERY, are you okay? You look like you're going to be sick."

I glanced over at Jordyn who was making us drinks in my kitchen. "Yes, I'm good. Just hoping that technically, everything works out tonight. Malakai went on two dates yesterday and one today. The cameraman, Steve, was supposed to get a little footage from each date."

That was a bold-faced lie, and judging by the way Jordyn rolled her eyes, she knew it, too. A couple nights ago, things with Malakai and I had gotten extremely out of hand and even though those delicious kisses were the best I'd ever had, making out with him right before he was scheduled to go on dates with other women was beyond wrong.

If my grandmother, Madea, could see me now, she'd strike me where I sit. I was raised better than this. My career was on the line and I truly did believe that this process could work for Malakai.

"Did you tell Tyler and Serenity what happened?" Jordyn asked, placing our drinks on my coffee table.

I laughed as I thought back to my quick conversation with Tyler and Serenity yesterday morning. "Girl, they were waiting at my desk when I got to the office. I didn't give them too many details. However, I told them we'd kissed, but agreed that he needed to continue with this process and go on the dates as if nothing happened."

Jordyn's eyebrows creased together. "So basically, you made them believe it was a mutual decision when Malakai clearly told you he's only going on these dates for you, but wasn't going to like it."

I waved her comment off. "Men will say anything when lust is doing all of the talking."

"Nah, I disagree. You didn't see how that man was looking at you when he got to the bar. And let's not forget how he was looking at you in his first live video. I don't know Malakai that well, but you do. Does he seem like the type of man to only let his dick do the talking?"

I thought about the man I'd been getting to know and the fact that even though he's known for being good in the bedroom, he didn't seem to be driven by his sexual needs.

"No, he doesn't." I glanced at the time on the corner of my laptop and saw the live video pop up in my Twitter feed. "It's starting."

True to what we'd discussed, Steve had gone on all three of Malakai's dates. The first fifteen minutes of the live video was a recap of all three dates. All three women were beautiful, and based off the clips, they seemed successful, too. The screen loved them and they each had chemistry with Malakai. Dr. Parker had done well with choosing the first three. *If she did so good, why does it make you feel like shit?* I knew why, but I had to accept the situation.

After the recap, Dr. Walker dove right into the session by asking Malakai some tough questions, including talking a little about how it was when he first began dating. I expected him to say he'd been dating multiple women from the age of fifteen or something like that, but what he said was the complete opposite.

"I'd never asked to be popular in high school," he said. "But I was, which meant that I was portrayed a certain way whether I wanted it or not. Don't get me wrong, I enjoyed high school, but I'd always felt a little different. Whereas most of the student body enjoyed going to football and basketball games, parades, and lived for homecoming and prom, I was the complete opposite. If I could stay in my room all day and just create something artistic, I was more than happy. Because I grew up with five brothers, I had no problem speaking my mind and shooting the shit, but when it came to dating, I was extremely shy."

"I can imagine that," Dr. Walker said. "You have a bold personality, but you also seem to be the type of man who appreciates the quiet moments."

As Malakai nodded his head, I thought about how much of a talker the first two dates were. On the surface, the dates seemed to go pretty well, but now listening to him, I was able to think back to what the camera had shown and realize that Malakai had seemed engaged, but the conversations had been pretty one-sided. Both women had done most the talking.

"I do appreciate those moments," Malakai agreed. "It takes a while for me to open up to a woman, and back in high school, it was even more difficult because they saw this popular guy with all of the friends. So, when we were alone and I'd rather talk about Leonardo da Vinci or painters who I wished the world knew more about like political painter and civil rights activist, Faith Ringgold, I would get a look like I was speaking a foreign language. Women needed an encyclopedia to understand me, so it didn't make it easy to be a misunderstood nerd." His laugh was boastful, but I could feel the slight pain between his vocal cords.

"It must have been difficult to be yourself," Dr. Walker remarked. "Studies show that a lot of social skills are developed in those pre-teen years and even earlier. Even though high school doesn't define us, depending on our experiences, it can be hard to find your footing."

The rest of the discussion with Dr. Walker and Malakai continued to pull me in. I couldn't stop watching it. Analyzing his words. Wondering if he meant what he said about his dates going well, or had they gone better and he just didn't want to say anything to jinx them.

My mind was reeling at how well that session had gone,

yet, it couldn't help but make me question what had happened between us a couple nights ago.

"Earth to Avery," Jordyn called, waving her hands in front of my face. "The video ended a couple minutes ago."

"Oh, right." I blinked my eyes a few times. "That was good, right?"

Instead of answering me, Jordyn shook her head as she took our empty glasses to my kitchen.

I stood from my couch. "What? You disagree?"

"I don't disagree," she said. "It really was good. But you can't tell me that you honestly think any of those women are better for him than you are?"

I glanced back down at my laptop as if the video would suddenly start replaying. *Were they? Was I?* "It doesn't matter because I have a job to do. I've already gotten three additional clients because news is traveling about me being hired by Malakai, so I have too much on my plate to even analyze the situation."

"Bullshit. If I know you, you're already analyzing it." She walked back to me and we both sat back down on the couch. "You know, for a woman who's never had an orgasm, you sure aren't getting that D as quickly as I wished you would."

My mouth dropped. "I'm not letting Malakai give me an orgasm."

"Girl, please. I bet you've been having freaky ass dreams about that man since you met him. Maybe even before because we all saw that dick pic. Listen," she began, her tone growing more serious, "you only told me a little bit about what you've gone through in the past when you lived in Tennessee, but word of advice, sis ... don't make up excuses as to why you can't be with that man."

I gave her a look of disbelief. "I don't know your entire

story about men you've dated in the past either, but based off what I know, isn't this the pot calling the kettle black?"

"Yeah, it is," she said, nodding her head. "But deep down, you know I'm right. All I'm saying is, let things happen however they should. Don't fight it." She waited a couple seconds before she went back to her antics. "And if you just so happen to trip into his bedroom and land right on his dick, then look at it like a sign from God that you need to tap that ass for all of the women in the world who wish they could."

I laughed so hard I could barely breathe.

TWELVE

Malakai

Lord, I promise if you let this date end early, I will go to church more. Hell, I was willing to donate all of my money to every charity in the area if it meant I could end this after dessert. As a matter of fact, I wasn't even sure I could get through dinner, let alone dessert.

I was on my fifth date, and even though Dr. Parker had found some great women, none of them were the women for me. None of them were Avery.

Avery. It had been almost two weeks since we'd kissed, and even though after the fifth day of avoiding me, I was still checking for her when Tyler not-so-subtly mentioned she was stopping by the office.

It was hard to believe that she'd been working with me for over a month already. She only stopped in the office periodically, and I'd learned from Serenity that she'd landed some other big clients as well. I was proud of her and happy that her agency was taking off and making a name for itself in New York. But the selfish part of me wished it was still during that trial period when she came into the office every day.

"And then, when I was seven, I got my first crush on a boy. His name was Tommy, I think. Then at age eight, I got my first group of close girlfriends. We would braid each other's hair and paint each other's nail. But nine was a great year ..."

I tried not to nod off as Cathy, my current date, continued to fill me in on each year of her life. The cameraman, Steve, was required to get enough footage to compose highlights for my sessions with Dr. Walker, but even he had left when she got to age four. For the life of me, I couldn't understand why ages one through six had been so damn long. I mean, how the hell do you even remember that much at that age? All I remember doing back then was napping, eating, pooping, and playing with my brothers. Cathy was over here talking about those years in detail, down to the coloring books she owned at that time.

"We're kindred spirits, Malakai. I know you feel it, too."

I tuned back into the convo when I heard my name. "Sorry, what was that?" I had to have heard her wrong. *Kindred spirits?* How in the world did she figure that?

"Our energies connect," she said, reaching over the table to grab my hand. "Just from touching you, I can feel a stronger force than I ever have. You have the spirit of a lion and I have the spirit of a deer. I'm your prey, Malakai. I'd be okay if you want to feed on me and give my remains to the rest of the wildlife."

"Uh ..."

"Don't fight it, Malakai." She gripped my hand tighter.

"I was born to let you chase me. Catch me. Kill me. Feed off me."

What the hell? I was two seconds away from snatching my hand from hers. I couldn't be sure, but it sounded like she'd suggested that I eat her? Either that, or she was suggesting I have sex with her and then share her with others like some twisted ménage-à-trois type shit.

"Cathy, I think we should end this date a little early." I went to pull my hand away, but she held on tight.

"Malakai, don't you see what I see? When my mother pushed me out of her vagina, the higher spirits deemed me as your sacrificial lamb." She stood from the table and came next to me, dropping to her knees. "I'm yours, Malakai," she yelled. "Do what you want with me. Do it, Malakai. Do it!"

"What the hell are you talking about?" By now, I was pulling my hand from hers, but when I did so, she grabbed both of my legs and wrapped herself around me. In my peripheral vision, I saw some people lift their cameras to record this craziness.

"That's Malakai Madden," I heard someone say.

"Oh, yeah. He's been dating to find his one true love," someone else commented.

"I think it's safe to say that she's not it," another remarked.

When our waiter came back to the table, I shot him and the guy sitting next to me with his old lady a look of desperation. Both came to my rescue, each trying to pry Cathy from my legs.

"You know I'm yours, Malakai. You must do it. We must complete our spiritual connection."

"Cathy," I said in the calmest voice I could muster, "please let me go so we can discuss what you're saying like adults. This isn't right."

"It is right." She was making her way farther up my body despite three of us trying to loosen her grip. After a few moments, the waiter and the other guy who was helping me gave up. I felt like a rag doll as she hung off me.

"Don't you understand, Malakai? I'm forty-one and I'm still single, but you get me, Malakai. Our spirit animals talk through us. You're weird just like me. I'm a nerd, too. I'm not accepted all of the time either."

I froze and stopped trying to break myself free. Somewhere between her yelling crazy things about spirit animals and clinging to me, I heard the pain in her voice. I heard the uncertainty that she would never find a person who understood her. I felt the disappointment that she hadn't found someone yet who was just as strange as she was. She was broken, and in more ways than one, I understand that.

"Cathy, stand up." I placed a comforting hand on her cheek, and in surprise, she loosened her grip and stood. Only then did I notice the tears running down her cheeks. I hadn't even realized she'd been crying.

"Hey, hey, hey," I murmured. "It's okay, Cathy. We've all been there. We've all had a time when we felt like no matter what we did, we couldn't change the way people viewed us."

She wiped her tears with the back of her hand. "Not you. At least, not in the same way as me. You're perfect. People don't look at you and think 'there goes the crazy cat lady.'"

I laughed to lighten the mood. "Not that exactly, but last year when all of that crazy stuff released on Twitter, I couldn't get people to see me as anything other than the Malakai Madden the media portrayed me to be. Sometimes, it's hard trying to be yourself, but you have to be. The world only made one you, so the best thing you can do is be the best version of yourself."

She glanced up at me, her brown eyes still watery from the tears. She was a beautiful woman, but there was hurt behind her eyes. "Thank you." She gave me a hug. "I'm sorry for how I behaved, and although I know this was probably our first and last date, I am really glad I got a chance to meet you."

I hugged her back, glad to finally meet the normal Cathy and not that spirit animal-crazed version of her. "You're welcome. Word of advice, though. On your next date, maybe start with telling the man about your current life instead of the past forty-one years first."

"Deal," she said with a laugh.

About ten minutes after our date had ended, Dr. Parker called me, apologizing for how the date had gone with Cathy even though I told her an apology wasn't necessary. I wasn't even surprised that videos of the scene had already surfaced on social media.

As I walked down the Manhattan streets, I couldn't keep my mind off Avery. So I decided to do what I always did when my mind was consumed with thoughts I couldn't control. Paint in one of my favorite places.

Avery

"THE WORLD only made one you, so the best thing you can do is be the best version of yourself."

I'd replayed one of the videos that surfaced online from

Malakai's date tonight about twenty times already, and every time I watched it, that line was still my favorite.

Leaning my head against the elevator, I waited to reach Malakai Madden Studios. Tyler had asked that I come tonight and insisted that whatever he had to tell me couldn't wait until I saw him in a couple days.

When I'd arrived at the building, the overnight security guard said he'd been expecting me and let me up. I wasn't sure what Tyler needed, but it better be good if it couldn't wait until a decent hour.

As the door opened, I glanced down at my black yoga pants, teal tank, and hoodie, wondering if I should have at least changed before I'd left my apartment.

"Screw it," I said aloud. "He called me out the bed at eleven at night."

While making my way to the doors leading to the offices, I noticed that the gallery door was open, although all of the lights were off.

"That's weird." The gallery door was never left open after hours and was often locked. I walked over to the door to close it, but was distracted by the faint sound of music in the background.

Maybe Tyler wanted to show me something in the gallery. I had walked through the gallery before, but I still hadn't gotten the chance to truly walk around like I wanted to. As I followed the sound of music, I took a chance to look at a few beautiful paintings and unique sculptures. The only light that allowed me to soak in the beauty of Malakai's creations were the designated spotlights on each piece of artwork.

"Breathtaking," I said, when I reached a sculpture of a woman whose head was turned upwards, while her arms wrapped around her body. *Heaven.* Such a beautiful name for this piece since it seemed as if she was looking up to heaven. You could almost feel her need to hug herself for protection against whatever was causing her to stand there in anguish. I'd seen a picture of the sculpture, but unlike a lot of Malakai's work, he'd never disclosed the meaning behind this one.

Moving along, I admired a few more pieces until the music grew louder. Turning a corner, I saw a door propped open at the end of a long hallway. I barely felt my feet move as I made my way to the room, my heart pounding in my chest at the thought that Tyler wasn't the person in that room. Malakai was. I felt it in the way my body was responding. In the way my toes were curling in my flip flops and the way my tank was getting tighter around my breasts. There was only one man who could garner such a strong reaction from me. One man who could make me feel as though he'd thoroughly fucked me with just one fiery gaze into my eyes.

When I reached the doorway, I froze. He was standing in the corner of the room in front of a painting that was about two feet taller than him. It appeared to be some sort of abstract piece with black and white being the dominant colors, but pops of brilliant colors throughout. I recalled Tyler saying Malakai had to finish an abstract piece for a music artist.

But the painting wasn't what was causing my mouth to water. Malakai's bare back was toward me and that alone was a sight I could never get tired of. His feet were bare and his muscular shoulders were bouncing to hip hop music that was coming through the speakers. Even though his hips weren't moving, my eyes were glued to the grey jogging pants that hung off his hips with a few paint stains on them. It made no sense for a man to have an ass that looked so delicious with clothes on. That meant if nothing was hiding my view, I could probably experience my first orgasm just from the sight of it.

I hadn't made a sound since I'd arrived, but suddenly, Malakai stopped moving. "I must have thought you up," he said as he lifted a remote to turn the music down a little. "How did you get in here?"

He still hadn't turned around, but I wasn't surprised he knew it was me. "Tyler asked me to meet him here for something. I was going to the offices to find him, but I noticed the door to your gallery open and when I went to close it, I heard the music playing."

"Tyler left a couple hours ago," he said, as he lifted his paintbrush and started painting again. "He was finishing up a project I'd asked him to work on when I arrived, but I told him to go home and get some rest."

That dude. Tyler was probably already at home when he'd texted me. "Sorry, I didn't know he wasn't here anymore." He didn't say anything, but continued painting. After a couple minutes of silence, I decided to leave.

"I didn't mean to bother you. I'll let you continue working the way you're used to."

"Can you tell what this is?" he asked, his back still toward me.

I studied the abstract painting more closely. It wasn't finished, but I could make out two faces. "Is it a man and woman?"

"Yes, it is," he said. "You can't tell yet, but they will both be wearing headphones. It's for a hip hop client I have. It's the last of a ten painting collection. It's a gift for his wife. His is the music we're listening to. Each painting represents a different part of their relationship." Malakai painted a few more lines.

"They met when they were in grammar school, way before his career took off. She's been there through every stage in his life, and despite the bad rep rappers get, their marriage is a strong and solid one. He and I ran into each at a restaurant in the Bronx where I was doing one of those 'live paintings in five minutes' type of competitions. He was the first hip hop artist who was willing to take a chance on me and my work."

"I remember reading about that," I said with a smile. "You were in your early twenties and hadn't been living in New York for that long. In the beginning of your career, you were doing anything you could to pay rent for the studio you had in Harlem. The best paintings you did were those with musical influence, but you were great at everything. I think you won about twenty competitions that year. Then a few years later, you decided to do a few more competitions. You lost a few, but you finally won one in Memphis, and after that, you were on fire."

He turned to me then, the view of his ripped abs causing my knees to buckle a bit. It wasn't until I noticed the curious look in his eyes that I'd realized I'd said too much. "Or so I've read," I said with a shrug.

Placing his paintbrush down, he crossed his arms over his chest and leaned on the wall next to the painting. "How much do you know about me?"

I shuffled from one foot to the other. "Not a lot," I lied. "But enough."

His eyes observed me, looking me up and down, the interest in his gaze leaving a heated path everywhere he looked. "I don't believe you." He pushed up from the wall and walked toward me. I began counting backward from ten in my mind to try and calm my nerves.

"How much do you know about me?" he asked again.

"And I'm not talking about things you could have read from an article."

Good job, Avery. When he'd first hired me to be his image consultant, he'd warned me about everyone who came before me. I knew admitting that I knew so much about him wouldn't go over well, but he deserved my honesty.

"I've been following your work since you won your first competition at sixteen," I said, ignoring the surprised expression on his face. "My Tennessee hometown was only about five hours away from yours, so when that local Arkansas college held those liberal arts awards for high school students, I was there visiting my older sister since she was attending the college. It was my freshman year, so I didn't know much about high school at the time, let alone college. But you looked so happy when you walked onstage to get your award. I had my sister take me to the student center right after the awards so I could see the painting you'd created."

"I can't believe you were there," he said, glancing down at my necklace. It seemed to briefly catch his interest and I wondered what that was about, but ignored it when he asked, "Was that the only time we were at the same place at the same time that you can recall?"

I bit my bottom lip. "Not exactly." I thought about how I could say I-had-a-crush-on-you-during-all-of-my-adolescence sound less like something crazy Cathy would say, but came up short. *I really shouldn't call her crazy Cathy.* Even though she and Malakai had ended their date on good terms, the memes and #CrazyCathy hashtag were already trending. My heart went out to her.

"Where?" he asked, breaking the direction of my thoughts. I sighed before responding.

"I was at your two Memphis painting competitions. By the time you did those shows, your name was beginning to float around and your work was being recognized." I thought back to those early years when I'd catch sight of him at certain art shows. "My sister used to tease me about the fact that I didn't even seem to care for art until I saw you my freshman year of high school. As an adult, I grew an even healthier appreciation for different art pieces, so when you opened your first gallery show here in New York, I was there amongst the hundreds of other people who'd shown up. You were twenty-three then, I think." He'd looked so happy that day. Nervous, but happy. "I hadn't even known you, but I was so proud to see how the sixteen-year-old artist that I'd followed since high school had managed to do so much in seven years. Your story was inspiring. Still is."

I was so wrapped up in remembering those times, I hadn't looked at Malakai in a while. When my eyes finally reached his, I couldn't read the expression on his face, which made me wonder if I'd shared too much. I was expecting for him to ask me if I could leave, but the words out his mouth were, "I'm going to kiss you. Unless you can give me a good reason why I shouldn't taste that sweet mouth of yours again."

"What?" I asked breathlessly. "You still want to kiss me?"

He took a few steps forward until I was close to the front of the room. Then, he closed the door and backed me into it. "There isn't a time when I don't want to kiss you," he said, right before his head dipped to mine.

The moment I felt his lips on mine, I dropped my purse to the ground and draped my arms over his shoulders. My entire body shook with desire when his tongue began to dance in my mouth just like it had the last time we kissed.

There were so many emotions running through my mind, that I could barely stand it. Here I was kissing the man who was the reason I loved art. The reason I couldn't pass an artist on a street corner without donating money toward his or her dream. The reason I knew the difference between watercolor acrylic and oil paint.

His hands played with the bottom of my hoodie until I reached up my arms so that he could peel it off. I expected him to go right back to kissing me, but instead, he stood back and studied my face. And it wasn't a quick study either. His hazel eyes were touching every part of my body, causing my nipples to grow harder under his stare and my sex to clench as if he were already inside of me.

We were going to have sex. I knew it. He knew it. Halo knew it because Coco was running the damn show. He stepped back to me and slowly rolled my tank off my body, exposing my breasts. Next, he slid off my yoga pants, giving me a moment to step out of them. When I was standing there in nothing but my black cotton panties, I couldn't remember the last time I'd been so naked. So exposed. We were high enough where no one could see us out of the window, but all the lights were still on even if they were a bit dimmed.

And the music was still playing, but his playlist was now on some smoother R&B music instead. I was nervous and excited at the same time. Nervous about what we were going to do because once we crossed that line, there was no turning back. But I was excited the man I'd fantasized about every time I imagined what an orgasm would feel like was standing right in front of me.

He began walking toward me with purpose. Determination. I prayed my nervous talking wouldn't kick in, but I knew I'd failed when I asked, "You're not just doing this because you overheard me say I've never had an orgasm before, right?" He froze and for a moment, I thought he hadn't heard what I'd said.

"Avery—"

"It's just, I don't want you to feel some false sense of responsibility or anything," I said cutting him off.

He shook his head. "You never feel like a responsibility."

"Good, because many women haven't had one."

He reached up to lightly touch my cheek. "You've never had an orgasm before?"

Crap. Way to go, Nightingale. I could have sworn he'd overheard that particular part at the bar, but he must have only heard the very last thing I said. "I thought that's what you'd overheard."

He gently rubbed circles on my right cheek with his thumb. "Avery, I heard you mention that you often imagined me naked and didn't know how you could ask me to give you an orgasm, but I didn't hear the part where you said you'd never had one. Had I known that, I never would have left your apartment that night."

I swallowed. "I promise you that despite everything I've revealed tonight, none of this stuff is the reason I wanted to be your image consultant."

"I know. But I have to ask. What do you want to happen tonight?"

What did I want to happen? Even though he knew my secret, I wasn't sure I had the courage to ask him for an orgasm. "It's been a while for me. As in, three years," I told him, studying his reaction.

"It's been a while for me, too," he said. "As in sixteen months."

I blinked my eyes in shock. Sixteen months seemed like

a long ass time for a man known to deliver multiple orgasms. Meaning, he was celibate for a reason. I didn't want to inter-fere with that reason, but I was tired of fighting it. Tired of denying it. Tired of wanting what I thought I shouldn't have.

"I want to have sex with you," I said, my eyes briefly dropping to his lips. "If that's what you want."

"It's what I want." Taking my hand, he kissed the back of it. In a flash, his eyes went from focused to intense making me wonder what I'd just agreed to. One thing I knew for sure—I was down for whatever the night may bring.

THIRTEEN

Avery

He led me to the other side of the room, the entire time his eyes holding mine. Out of nervousness, I glanced around the entire space for the first time, taking note of the half-done sculpture in a corner and different artistic designs scattered throughout.

There was something about being in his creative space that felt intimate and sacred. I'm sure he'd shown this space to others before, but it felt private. Like I was the only one he'd ever showed.

When my feet hit something soft on the floor, I almost tripped on the mattress pad and blankets scattered around, until Malakai gripped me around my waist to keep me steady.

"I've fallen asleep in here more times than I can count," he said, before nodding to his right. "There's a bathroom and shower over there, so if I didn't want to leave, I wouldn't have to. I'm sure you notice how many random beds are on this floor."

I smiled as I thought about the empty office and his office which both had futons. "Well, it's better to have a place to sleep so you can still be creative, rather than leave and possibly disrupt your inspiration."

"I couldn't agree more." He lifted my chin so that my lips were better angled with his. "Except for a few times, I usually have really good intuition." His eyes slowly glanced over my naked breasts and black panties before dropping to my lips. "But I didn't see you coming."

"That makes two of us," I said, my voice low with desire. I'd often thought about what I would do if I was able to have a moment alone with Malakai, but never in my wildest dreams did I think we'd be in this place, now, in this moment.

"You're beautiful as hell." His hazel eyes darkened to a deeper brownish-green, the color and the transition causing me to drag my bottom lip between my teeth. Leaning down close to my ear, he whispered, "I want you to savor this moment for as long as I can, but I'm not sure how long I can hold off fucking you senseless." His breath tickled my neck. "Or seeing just how sweet this pussy of yours tastes on my tongue."

My knees almost buckled beneath me at his words. Then, in a move I should have been ready for, but wasn't, he eased me down to the mattress pad and slid my panties down my hips, placing kisses along my thighs and calves before he removed them completely.

Still on his knees, he leaned back, dragging a finger in between my breasts, down to my core. *Oh, God.* My breath hitched when his hands found my clit, before dragging his fingers over my core and lips. His strokes were soft and unhurried. Precise, yet, he hadn't even done much yet.

"I remember reading a study years ago that said about seventy percent of women have never reached an orgasm during intercourse." He kissed my lower stomach and inner thighs, spreading my legs open more as he did so.

"That same study said thirty-five percent never experience an orgasm during oral sex." He placed a soft kiss on my clit, and just the feel of his breath on the most sensitive part of my body caused me to buck under his mouth.

I sighed as he made his way up my body, leaving the part that was aching for him most.

"Just to clarify, you've never had an orgasm?"

"Right," I replied, studying his eyes. "I've reached an orgasm on my own, but never with a man. I think when it gets to that point, I overthink things."

He sweetly kissed my lips before he went back down between my legs. "For a man, the key is to make a woman feel so cherished ... so beautiful, that the only thought on her mind is one of pure, unadulterated pleasure."

His words were beautiful, and whatever response had been on the tip of my tongue, died the moment I felt his tongue back on my clit. Only this time, the kisses weren't light and sweet. More like, purposeful and determined. His tongue swirled around my nub in a way I'd never felt before. The twists and turns made my back arch from the sheets as he dipped his tongue into my aching center, moving in the same motions he had on my clit.

"Oh, shit." My voice a muffled mess, and even though cursing was nowhere near as poetic as the way he was making me feel, I had every word in the dictionary flashing across my mind as I felt a heightened awareness that I'd never felt before.

As his tongue stroked me even further into a lustful cocoon, I thought about the fact that without any use of fingers like other men had previously tried to use to get me to orgasm, he was coaxing out all of my pleasure with just one body part.

It almost seemed unfair that a man possessed a tongue so thick and long, that it had me hitting those high notes of the current song that was playing and I knew I couldn't sing worth a damn.

I bucked a few more times until he caught my ass in his hands and kept me pinned to his mouth. *What. The. Fuck.* I was starting to lose feeling in my legs because the buildup of passion was too fierce. A part of me, who I assumed to be Coco, was telling me to enjoy every second of this beautiful tongue attached to this sexy man and ride on the orgasm I knew was near. However, the other part of me, Halo my good and reasonable conscious, was warning me that letting him be my first orgasm was a bad idea. I needed to remain in control of this situation and I was losing control. Fast.

"Malakai," I panted as his tongue increased its move-ments. I could feel it coming in every bone of my body and before I knew what was happening, I was wailing his name and shaking uncontrollably as I released a powerful orgasm that felt so strong, I was sure it rattled the entire floor. Yet, his tongue didn't stop there.

In an expert move, he flipped onto his back, turning me over with him and keeping his tongue buried deep inside of my pussy. I squirmed, still convulsing from my orgasm and trying to find some relief, when he coaxed me into another one before I could even figure out what was going on. I bucked again, riding his face as he licked all my juices and kept up with the rhythm I had set.

After I came down from my high, I expected Malakai to

BLESSED BY MALAKAI   125

give me a moment to regain composure, but that wasn't the case. He spun me back around so that I was on my back again and stood, removing his jogging pants in a way that was just as smooth as everything else about him.

"There it is," I said aloud as I stared at the dick that starred in more than a few sex dreams. He laughed, and I covered my mouth in embarrassment that I'd said my previous words aloud. But I couldn't help it. I wasn't the type that enjoyed looking at the male anatomy, but clearly, that was before I'd seen Malakai.

The pictures that had been floating around the internet didn't do this man justice. I leaned on my knees and reached out my hands to touch it, unable to keep them to myself any longer. *Mouthwatering.* That was the only word I could use to describe it. It was the same brown-cinnamon color as the rest of him and the sight had me closing my mouth to make sure I didn't drool. *Damn.* I hadn't had sex with a lot of men, but it didn't take an overly experienced woman to know that his dick wasn't like the others. His shaft was thick, causing me to push away the fear that he was too big to fit. *Girl, you'll make it work.*

But it wasn't just his thick shaft that had me panting. It wasn't until he'd removed his pants that I realized I'd never been with a man with that naturally curved tip that I'd read about before. It was so long, it didn't just stick straight out when he got hard. Nope, not at all. It had the type of slight hook that promised to leave a lifetime of pleasure wherever he touched and I swear the tip winked at me as I got closer to it. My mouth was eager to just sample a quick taste.

My lips had barely been able to wrap about the tip, when Malakai leaned down to put on protection before gently laying me back down to the mattress pad. I opened my mouth to protest because I really did want to enjoy tasting him for a bit, when he placed a heated kiss on my lips at the same time that he entered my body.

Slowly, he edged into me, each inch filling me with more pleasure than the last. Any thoughts I'd previously had were erased the moment he'd filled me completely.

"Fuck," he said, leaning above me. "You feel amazing." I could see the lines straining his forearms as he held himself up, gazing into my eyes as he began to move inside of me. He'd barely gotten started and I was already moaning loudly, but I didn't care. I had too many emotions floating around to keep anything inside.

Every movement of his body seemed to dance in a unique rhythm that was all Malakai. His thrusts were stroking my body as if I were a blank canvas, waiting for him to paint a breathtaking picture. His eyes staring down at mine were speaking to a part of my body and soul that I didn't even know was there.

My mind couldn't make sense of it, but every move made me feel unhinged. We didn't need words. Words were unnecessary in defining a moment so exhilarating, that I almost cried in pity for any man who would touch me after him. Malakai Madden wasn't just making love to my body and soul. He was painting an entire picture with strokes so deep, they rose from the art piece. Lines so precise, each one evoked a new emotion depending on the person viewing the painting.

At times, it felt like we were making love like we were the last two people on Earth. Then other times, he was fucking me senseless and there was nothing sweet and gently about it. He sexed my body in a way that was graceful yet unforgiving, and when he angled my right leg to get even deeper, I felt us reach another level of intimacy.

His name left my lips again as I grew closer and closer

to another orgasm, completely undone by the fact that this was going to be my third one. I'd heard some women say they saw stars when it happened. Others said fireworks. I once had a friend who said good sex made her weep in pleasure.

Well, now I knew my trigger and even though it was probably the most unsexy thing I could imagine, Malakai made me come so hard that I sounded as if I was speaking tongue. I couldn't make out a word I was saying, which meant, he probably couldn't understand anything either. Instead of making me feel stupid, he smiled that sexy smile of his and released his orgasm soon after, whispering my name over and over as he did.

He didn't roll off me right away, but once he went to the bathroom to discard the condom, I finally got a moment to get myself together. I ran my fingers through my hair and shook my legs in excitement. *Holy mother of Pearls.* I couldn't believe I'd just experienced my first three orgasms.

Malakai had done what no man had ever done. He'd fucked me so good, no man from my past even came in as a close second. There were so many reasons why I needed to throw on my clothes, find my purse, and get my ass back home. But that's not what I did. Instead, when he returned and sweetly kissed my neck, I kissed him back. When he began sucking my nipples, I held his head closer and savored his warm mouth. When he got in between my legs and looked at me with those fuck me eyes, I dropped my legs farther apart, anticipating that we were going to go another round. And just like the last round, he didn't hold anything back.

FOURTEEN

Malakai

For the first time, I did something that I hadn't done in over a year. I played hooky and decided to spend the entire day in bed doing nothing.

Except, I wasn't the only person playing hooky today. As I glanced over at the sleeping beauty next to me, I mouthed a silent thank you to whoever was looking out for me and managed to get Avery to agree to come back to my place after we'd left the gallery in the wee hours of the morning.

Last night had completely rocked my world just the way I knew it would. I'd waited over a year to be inside of a woman and I was damn sure happy I had. Being buried deep inside of Avery was a feeling I couldn't describe and one that I had never felt before. It was almost like our bodies were speaking together in a way much stronger than normal. We moved together like a slow love song and connected better than the perfect color combination on a white canvas.

And you were her first orgasm. I still couldn't get over that shit. I knew how blessed I was to have been the man to give her such a release. She'd deserved twenty orgasms last night, but a man could only do so much in the time they'd had. I hoped she realized that it was going to be difficult for me to refrain from giving her an orgasm every time I was around her. The way I saw it, we had to make up for the lost time she'd wasted on those other cats who hadn't gotten the job done. *Waste of fucking space on men who could leave a woman unsatisfied, but make sure they get theirs.*

After we'd had sex the first time, we had sex twice more until succumbing to sleep for an hour, only to wake up after Tyler repeatedly knocked on the door at 5 a.m. to let us know that some of the early folks were due to arrive at the office in the next hour.

He gave us privacy while we gathered ourselves and snuck out down the exit stairs, but before he'd gone, I thanked him for looking out. So in a way, I guess Tyler was one of those people who'd made it possible for Avery to be with me right now.

I glanced at her again, her body rising and falling under the blue sheet. She'd been sleeping for the past six hours, and although I'd love to let her get more rest, breakfast was getting cold and I knew she needed some nourishment to replenish her energy.

When I sat on the edge of the bed, the sheet slightly slipped from her naked body, giving me a better view. Her body was a work of art, each part telling a story of where she'd been. What she'd done. I wanted to know if the scar on the back of her right calf was from her adolescence or adult years. I kissed the dark freckles on her stomach and chest, which matched the ones sporadically sprinkled on her face. The ones that many probably missed because they'd never observed her as closely as I had. I rubbed the stretch marks along her thighs, loving the fact that they symbolized a thick, curvy woman. A real woman. A girl who'd grown into her womanhood and denounced society's standards, by instead symbolizing the true definition of a beautiful black queen.

I gently ran my fingers through her luscious curls that currently weren't pulled back or restrained by any ponytail holders, but rather, they were wild and free just like the woman they belonged to. My fingers then traced her black feather tattoo on the back of her left shoulder, my eyes unable to stop staring at it.

She knows your journey. Better yet, I had a feeling she was my journey. Or at least a path I had to take to get to where I needed to be in life. When Avery had mentioned all of the times she'd seen me before and followed my career ever since I was sixteen, I could tell she was apprehensive and worried that it would freak me out. Little did she know, it had done quite the opposite. My soul recognized her words for what they meant the minute she'd said them. Only, despite all of the steps we'd taken in our relationship last night, I knew she still needed to be convinced that she and I belonged together. She wasn't just a part of my journey ... I was also a part of hers.

"Rise and shine, beautiful." I placed a soft kiss on the temple of her forehead, before moving to her lips to tempt her awake.

"Hmm. Malakai, I have morning breath," she said between kisses.

"I don't give a damn." I deepened the kiss, pulling her up and into my arms as I did so. After a couple minutes, I finally ended the kiss. "I laid out a new toothbrush in the bathroom and you can use whatever I have in my bathroom that you want."

She rubbed her sleepy eyes and glanced at the clock on the nightstand. "Shouldn't you be at work right now?"

"I told Tyler to let the others know I wouldn't be in today and to reschedule any meetings."

She nodded her head as she glanced around again. "Your loft is amazing. It's exactly the type of place I pictured you would have."

My loft was three levels, and although the third level held two private bedrooms with connecting bathrooms, I'd chosen the bedroom loft on the second floor that overlooked my first floor.

Most of my place was brick and wood, which was exactly how I liked it. Artistic paintings and sculptures that I'd done, or were done by close friends in the industry, were stationed throughout my entire place.

I tossed Avery a grey T-shirt before she made it to the bathroom and waited for her to brush her teeth. Forgetting about the food, I knocked and told her she could shower after if she wanted, but that I'd made her breakfast.

"This is so sweet," Avery remarked as she took a seat at my paint-splattered kitchen table. "I don't think a man has ever made breakfast for me before."

I shook my head. "I'm disappointed in some of the men out there," I said, placing the orange juice, eggs, toast, fruit, and chicken apple sausage on the table I'd set earlier. "What happened to catering to a woman by waking her up to sex and breakfast?"

"I don't know," she replied with a laugh. "But I'm glad you still practice that rule." She was looking at the wooden placemats I'd carved when I took a seat across from her at the table.

"I love how unique everything in your place is."

"Thank you." I took a bite of the chicken apple sausage. "Every piece has a purpose and every section of this place has a story. Painting and sculpting are how I make a living, but I don't want to ever forget how much fun I have creating pieces that may never make it into my gallery or aren't for a client."

Avery took a bite of her eggs. "I was never much of a graphic designer or anything, but my sister and I used to create jewelry for fun. She actually designs and sells jewelry back in Tennessee at her shop, but her and I haven't created anything in a long time."

"Why not?"

Her face grew solemn. "We haven't spoken in over three years," she answered in a sad voice. "I guess I haven't felt the urge to create anything if we aren't doing it together."

I didn't want to pry, but I curious about the rest of the story. "Why haven't you spoken in so long? Family argument? I assume it's over something serious."

"It is." She moaned. "Ugh, I'm sorry. This is so not the type of conversation we should be having after the body-numbing sex we had all night."

"I disagree." After putting down my fork, I reached for her hand. "I want to know all about you, Avery. That includes the parts of your life that may not be so sunshine and rainbows. Hell, I know I've got shit that I hate talking about, but for you, I'd give it a try. So if you're willing, I will, too."

Her eyes softened and she squeezed my hand back. "Thanks for that." Leaning back in her chair, she took a deep breath. "Although I've always been close to my parents and my sister, I haven't seen my sister in over three years because she fell in love with my ex-fiancé while we were still engaged. They just got married two years ago.

"Damn," I muttered, unable to help myself. "That's fucked up."

"Yeah, it is." She shuffled some food around on her plate. "Back in Tennessee, I worked as a PR consultant at the top PR firm in the south. My ex, Julian, worked there in operations. He asked me out my second week working at the company and I guess you can say we fell in love fast. Too fast now that I think about it. I've always been particular with who I introduce to my family, so he didn't meet my family until we'd already been dating six months.

"When I introduced him to my sister, Vanessa, I'd noticed the look of recognition in both his eyes and my sister's, but when I asked if they knew each other, they denied it. For a while, I questioned my sister about it and she kept denying it. Therefore, to ease my own mind, I decided to do a little research and discovered they had both attended the same sports camp every summer. When I brought it up to my sister then, she told me they had known each other, but didn't get along. When my ex had the same story, I let it go.

"Two more years passed and Julian proposed. I accepted, convinced he was the right guy for me. According to my sister, they had sex the night he proposed. She claims they only had sex twice throughout the course of our relationship, but she conveniently thought the best time to give me this fucked up news was two weeks before my wedding."

"That is so messed up." Shaking my head, I took a sip of my orange juice. "Didn't Julian put two and two together before he met your sister because of your last name?"

"Vanny and I have different last names. My mom was with her father before she met my father. Her dad passed away and my mom met my dad who fell in love with my mom and her daughter. They got pregnant with me after only being together for a few months and married after I was born. Vanny is seven years older than me and my parents are celebrating their thirtieth anniversary this fall."

"So you call your sister Vanny? That's her nickname?"

"Yeah, it is," Avery said with a strained laugh. "Her full name is Vanessa Marie Straton. Julian knew her as Nessa Marie because that's what she went by every summer in camp. Vanny and Julian are about the same age." She grew quiet and had this faraway look in her eyes. I was about to tell her she didn't have to talk about it anymore if she didn't want to, but she continued.

"The funny thing is, I'm not upset that Julian and Vanny didn't tell me that they knew each other and dated every summer for five years. I'm not even upset that they are happily married now."

"You're not?" I asked, studying her face. "Because it's understandable if you are. Especially since you haven't spoken to your sister in over three years. I'm not sure I could handle that if one of my brothers married a woman I loved."

"I know it sounds strange," she said, "but I'm more upset that they had an affair when he and I were still together more so than any of my other stuff." She looked me in the eyes. "When I look back on the time Julian and I spent together, all I see is everything that had been missing in our relationship. Even though we have differences and don't look alike because we both take after our fathers, Vanny and I are a lot alike. I know now that the parts of me that Julian liked were the parts that reminded him of the girl he'd fallen in love with who he lost contact with once the sports camp closed. Social media wasn't around back then, and neither of them are on social media today. Vanny didn't even have a cell phone because they were just becoming popular. Their story was one of a love lost that was found again, but in this case, the person who helped them find each other was me, someone they both loved, but hurt in the process of reconnecting with one another."

She smiled. "I want them to be happy, and when my parents tell me they are, it makes me smile. But it's just so strange being around them after everything that's happened."

Instead of my heart aching for Avery, it grew in pride at the fact that even though she was the person they'd both hurt and disappointed by having an affair behind her back, she still wanted them to be happy. She was glad that they'd found their happily ever after, even if that meant she'd been hurt in the process. "You're an amazing woman." Lifting her hand, I brought it to my lips. "Some woman would say that they wanted to slash the tires of his favorite car or cut his dick off in his sleep if their man was cheating on her."

"Oh I thought about slashing his tires," she said with a laugh. "His tires and my sister's, but I never did. And I'd never cut his dick off because even though this situation is awkward as hell, he needs his dick so he can give my sister some babies. She's wanted to be a mom her entire life, so I know she's probably anxious to start their family."

"See, that's what I mean." I looked at her in awe. "Still thinking about what's best for them. Tell me again why you haven't spoken to your sister in three years? I know they hurt you, but you seem to be healing."

"I have healed." She sighed. "Marrying Julian would have been a mistake and I'm so glad I didn't. Granted, I couldn't wait to get out of Tennessee and it took a little longer than I would have liked to get to New York, but I'm not the same Avery Nightingale I was a few years ago. They don't know this, but there were a couple times I was out with friends and I saw them on a date. They were so in love, and I'd never seen my sister look at any man like that. I'd also never seen Julian look at me the way he did my sister.

"Watching them, I had also remembered the stories my sister used to tell me about a boy she called JJ who she looked forward to seeing every summer. Even said he was her first love. Julian's middle name was Jeremy. Once I pieced even more together, I got angrier for a little while and told my parents I wasn't celebrating any holidays with them if Vanny was there. Therefore, my parents choose to celebrate separate holidays with us. One daughter for Christmas, the other for Thanksgiving. Alternating every year. Honestly, I forgave them probably a year after it happened and realized that maybe fate used me as a medium to bring them together. So yeah, I'm over it. I just don't know how to approach the situation."

I shrugged. "I think you approach it from the heart. As you've said, you've had time to heal and you forgave them a while ago. I agree, the situation is incredibly awkward, but I have a feeling that reconciling won't be as difficult as you think it will. Avery, you're great with bringing people together. Everyone at the office loves you. Hell, everyone you meet seems to want to be around you all of the time. Present company included." I smiled, loving the way her lips slightly opened in a soft gasp. "Maybe you should just call your sister one day. You don't have to have a heart-to-heart about what happened. At least not at first. But I bet your sister would love to hear from you and misses you."

"I miss her, too." Avery's eyes were misty. "I think you're right. Maybe I'll call her sometime this week. Family is important, and regardless of what happened in the past, I want to move forward."

We resumed eating, conversation flowing between us as effortlessly as everything else had been. Avery agreed to spend the day with me, but she'd declined my offer to take her to dinner, reminding me that I had to take out a couple of the women Dr. Parker had paired me with.

I nodded my head as if I agreed, but I didn't. Not even a little. There was no way in hell I was dating those other women when I knew the only woman I wanted was sitting across from me. I had made a commitment to have the online sessions with Dr. Walker and I would. Talking to him was therapeutic even if it was in front of thousands of people. Even though I'd made a commitment with Dr. Parker as well, I had a feeling that I owed her a call to explain my situation and pray that she'd help me find a creative way to get out of my remaining dates so I could focus my attention on Avery without her freaking out.

FIFTEEN

Avery

"I'm such a homewrecker," I cried, dropping my head to the table. With the exception of a couple meetings I'd had at Malakai's office, I hadn't been alone with him since I'd left his place. My emotions were at an all-time high, so I figured I needed to call my friends to talk shit out. I'd always been fine with sharing, and Tyler, Serenity, and even Jordyn—who usually didn't pry—had each called or texted me for details of what happened after Tyler had found us in Malakai's gallery.

"How so?" Serenity asked. "Malakai isn't married."

"Don't you get it? I'm wrecking it for the future Mrs. Madden since it's been a week and he hasn't gone out on any night dates with any of the remaining two women. Only lunch dates."

"How is that a problem?" Jordyn inquired. "I thought you liked Malakai. Especially since he finally popped your orgasm cherry. Why do you still want him to go out on dates?"

"I don't still want him to go on dates," I lifted my head. "But 'Malakai Madden's Journey to Love' was my idea, so he has to see it through."

"I still don't know why you suggested this," Tyler said, returning from the bathroom. "You already knew y'all had crazy chemistry before you put the plan in motion."

"I know." I thought back to the meeting I'd had with Malakai when I initially presented my idea. "Deep down, I think that's why I'd decided to go through with the idea. Our chemistry was so strong, I couldn't handle the heat."

"Speaking of heat," Jordyn began, "was the sex as good as you thought it would be?"

Just as it did whenever I thought about sex with Malakai, my heart started beating twice it's normal rate. Last week, we'd spent two days sexing each other crazy, only taking breaks to talk and eat. "It was better than I thought it would be. Sex with Malakai wasn't just about the act. It felt like he'd known my body forever. And he hadn't just been talking to my body. He'd been talking to my heart... my soul. As cheesy as it sounds, he had my nose and legs wide the fuck open and all I could do was give him whatever he wanted."

"Damn," Jordyn said.

Tyler winked. "When y'all get married and start having babies, don't forget who helped make the best sex of your lives happen."

"That's some deep shit." Serenity's voice was dreamy as she spoke.

"I know." I fidgeted with the straw in my drink. "Did you guys see tonight's live Twitter session with Malakai and Dr. Walker?"

"Of course we did," Tyler said. "We assumed that's why you wanted to meet tonight."

"It was. I thought tonight's session, which focused a lot on his family and the fact that he wants a love like his parents who have been married for almost forty years, was extremely touching."

"It was." Jordyn smiled. "I'm not even into all that soft, emotional shit. But he had me dabbing the corners of my eyes at his words."

"You know what else I noticed?" Serenity began with a sneaky smile. "I noticed that the reflection of his dates was really PG. It seemed more to me like he was catching up with two friends than having romantic lunch dates."

Tyler nodded his head. "I agree with Serenity. He had nothing but nice things to say about both women, but did anyone else peep the fact that everything he said seemed to be just on the surface? Like a friend who was trying to make another friend sound good so they could hook them up."

"I don't even know Malakai that well, but even I noticed that," Jordyn said.

The table grew quiet as they each waited for me to mention if I'd noticed the same thing. "Yeah, I noticed," I admitted. "Not sure what it means though."

"Well," Serenity smiled, "maybe you should ask him."

I was about to tell them that I didn't have the guts to do that when my phone rang. A quick glance proved that it was the man of the hour. I placed my phone back down as if it were lighting my hand on fire.

"Answer it," Tyler encouraged.

Instead of listening to him, I stared at the phone a little longer.

"It's not going to answer itself." Jordyn gestured her hands as if to tell me to answer it now.

I cleared my throat. "Hi, Malakai."

"Avery. Avery. Avery." Each time he said my name was deeper than the last. "I have a favor to ask you."

"Sure," I replied, smiling in spite of myself. "What do you need?"

"I know this is short notice, but this weekend, I have to go to Cranberry Heights, my hometown. My parents are having their annual summer barbecue and I was hoping that you could accompany me."

My mouth slightly parted. "Wow, I'm honored that you asked me."

He laughed. "Is that a yes?"

"Uh." I didn't have any plans this weekend, but it seemed weird for me to go to his hometown and meet his family. Did he want me to go as a friend? As a girlfriend? Fake girlfriend? Image consultant? "Are you sure that's a good idea? Didn't you have any dates scheduled this weekend? Maybe you want to bring one of them?"

"No, I want to bring you. I want to show you my hometown and introduce you to my family."

Okay, so that didn't really help me decide which category I fell into, but I wasn't sure it mattered. I wanted to say yes even though I knew I should probably decline.

"Pretty please," he said in an adorable voice. "I really want to show you off. Plus, Crayson and Serenity are coming, so you'll know some other people there if you're worried about that."

"I'm not worried about that," I assured. "Okay, I'll go with you."

"Great." His voice held promise. "I'm looking forward to it."

We discussed a few more details before we disconnected our call.

"I assume from that dreamy-eyed expression on your face that you told him you'd go to the barbecue at his parents' place in Arkansas?" Tyler questioned.

"You knew he was going to ask me to go?"

Tyler shrugged. "Maybe. I've gone to the barbecue for the past few years, but I have something with my own family this weekend, so I'll be headed to LA."

"I'll be there though," Serenity said. "The Madden family always invites the entire town to the festivities they have on Saturday."

"I'm glad you'll be there." I smiled. "I'm not sure what to expect and I'm hoping folks don't think we're together. I'll probably need at least one friend who knows the truth."

The smile on Serenity's face should have made me more nervous, but it didn't. I couldn't have any more butter-flies swarming through my stomach than I currently did. My friends finally started talking about something else and paying me little mind.

I was a nervous wreck, so I had to get my shit together. The best thing I could do for myself was to try not to think about Malakai before I absolutely had to. Therefore, I had two days to get everything into perspective.

It's a little late for that, Avery. You're already falling in love with him. I closed my eyes at the realization that shouldn't have even been as surprising to me as it was. If I were honest with myself, I'd admit that I knew I'd fallen in love with him the minute he offered me the job as his image consultant. If I were honest with myself, I'd admit that there wasn't any man in this world who made me feel the way that Malakai did. If I were honest with myself, I'd admit that a part of me fell in love with him when I was fourteen and he didn't know I existed, so knowing the man that I knew now, my love for him had only heightened. Intensified. Consumed my mind and body with feelings and emotions that I hadn't even known I had.

I'd always been a secure person, even if the world gave me reason to lack my securities. However, in this moment, the feeling of insecurity was creeping into my mind and heart faster than I could stop it. And I needed to stop it. I couldn't let it *or him* consume me.

Avery

"THAT BITCH COCO," I huffed as I pushed back the covers on my bed and groaned after having yet another sex dream about Malakai. Some people didn't dream hard enough for it to fuck up their day. Unfortunately for me, I was one of those people who remembered their dreams in detail.

For the past forty-eight hours, I had been telling Coco to plant her horny ass in the back of my mind and not to come out unless I called for her. I told her that the past two days were all about Halo because Halo understood that I needed to free my mind of thoughts of Malakai Madden. Halo knew that I needed a break from my psyche if I was ever going to get anything done. Halo knew that a true bitch had your back no matter what, which meant, anything related to Malakai Madden had been put on pause until I met him at the airport.

Instead of listening to me, Coco had decided that she didn't want Halo to be in charge. Coco had decided that

Malakai deserved a permanent spot in my mind. In my heart. In my bed. *Damn her*.

Although he'd eventually said okay to meeting me at the airport instead of picking me up, I was still nervous to see him soon. However, that wasn't the only thing I was nervous about. It was long overdue, but I was going to call my sister after three long years of not voicing a word to one another. I was finally calling Vanny.

After I brushed my teeth, got in the shower and got dressed, I made sure my suitcase was packed and reached for my phone to FaceTime her. By the time the phone was on the third ring, I was ready to hang up when Vanny's surprised face filled the phone.

"Avery, I can't believe you're calling me." She smiled, her eyes darting across the screen as if she were imagining this moment.

"Hey Vanny," I said. "I know this call may be random, but I figured it was long overdue."

"I was willing to wait three or more years to talk to you if it meant my little sis would eventually call," she said. "I've missed you so much."

"I've missed you, too." I smiled as Vanny's eyes got watery. "I was talking to a friend the other day about how much I miss creating jewelry with you, too."

"Oh my gosh, me too," Vanny said. "My best-selling pieces at the shop have all been designs that we've come up with together. None of my stuff in the past couple years sells as well. You always were my inspiration." Frowning, she wiped a couple tears. "Avery, words can't express how sorry I am for what I did to you. You were more than just my sister. You were one of my best friends. It may not mean much to you, but Julian and I talk all the time about what terrible people we are for what we did. You have always been one of the most selfless people I know and I don't deserve your love, but damn, sis, I want you back in my life. I have no right to ask and you have every right to say no, but I need you back in my life, Avery."

"I need you in mine, too." I sniffled back my own tears. "A part of me feels like something is missing without you. But I'm not going to lie. It's going to be really strange seeing you and Julian together. And it may even hurt more than I expect it to. But I know being in your life means I'll have to get used to it."

"I'll do whatever it takes to rebuild our relationship and earn your trust back," Vanny's tears flowed more freely. "You may never fully forgive me, but trust me, I will never ever forgive myself for what I did."

"I forgive you, Vanny," I said. "I forgive Julian, too. I did a long time ago, but every time I thought about telling you, I decided not to."

"You had every right to take whatever time you needed. I'm just glad that you called me today. Especially since when I got this news, you were the first person I wanted to call."

My eyes widened in surprise. "Oh my God, you're pregnant! Aren't you?"

Vanny nodded her head. "I am. Only a month. Not even Julian knows yet." She squinted her eyes. "Is that okay? Or should I have not shared that?"

"It's fine," I told her, truly meaning it. "I'm happy for you." Even though I loved hearing the excitement in my sister's voice, as I'd figured, the conversation did hurt a little. There was no way we would ever have the same relationship we used to have, but I was willing to give a new relationship a try. I only had one sister and regardless of how much I still didn't care too much for my sister's husband

and my ex-fiancé, I wanted to be in my niece or nephew's life.

The last thought I had as I ended the call with my sister was once again about Malakai. *I'm glad he convinced me to call.* And it wasn't that I was glad for my sister's sake. I was glad I'd called for my own sake.

SIXTEEN

Malakai

Damn, she's so beautiful. Seeing Avery in my hometown was doing crazy things to my state of mind. I loved my parents' annual summer party, but I was finding it hard to focus with Avery around.

On the plane ride down a few hours ago, Avery had slept the entire flight. Either that or she was pretending to sleep to avoid talking to me. When we'd arrived at my parents' B&B, I had barely introduced her to everyone in the room, before they were pulling her in every direction and telling her all about the Friday fish fry they were having in town.

"Are you going to keep watching her all day, or are you going to actually join in on our conversation?" Crayson asked, breaking me from my thoughts.

"I know that look," my brother, Micah, said.

"Yep," Malik agreed. "Me too. It's the look of a man who can't keep his mind off a particular woman."

"One of y'all has to fill me in," my brother, Caden, said.

Crayson and Caden made up two-thirds of the triplets. My only brother that wouldn't be in attendance was Carter, but that wasn't unusual. Carter was in the military and had been living around the world since he was eighteen. So, the few times he popped into town were random, but when he did, we all dropped what we were doing to fly back home and see him.

"I thought Malakai was dating multiple women on Twitter or something like that? When did he start dating his image consultant?" Caden asked.

Caden was the only brother still living in Cranberry Heights, but had also spent some time in the military. Malik, Micah, Crayson, and I all preferred city living, but not Caden. Modern-aged cowboy would best describe him and his style of living.

"I'm not dating the women Dr. Parker set me up with," I said. "At least not anymore."

"Malakai was feeling Avery when he first met her during her interview," Crayson said. "Malik and I knew then that he wasn't going to keep his hands off her."

Caden raised an eyebrow. "It's like that, bruh? Sleeping with your consultant."

"It's more than that," I stated, brushing off his words. "Y'all already know that all of this Twitter mess started when I told crazy Roxanne that I was looking to settle down."

I glanced over at Avery who was laughing at something that Serenity or one of my sisters-in-law had said. "She doesn't know it yet, but Avery is it for me, fellas. If she'll have me, I plan to wife her up."

As if she knew we were talking about her, she turned to look my way and our eyes caught. She smiled at me and waved, and as I returned the sentiment, I was already secretly thanking my parents for placing our rooms right next to each other. I'd almost told them that one room was fine, but hadn't wanted to embarrass her.

"Speaking of Roxanne, why hasn't she been popping up lately?" Crayson asked. "She's usually all over New York tracking you. With all that mess with Antoine, I missed the story."

I shook my head. "I had to get a restraining order after she snuck her way into the office a week after the Twitter mess. She was waiting in my office butt ass naked. The cameras in the building caught everything. She apologized, and last I heard, she was dating an NBA player who played for the Bulls."

"We see her in Chicago from time to time," Malik said. "Her new guy and I have a mutual friend who said that he's in love with Roxanne and will probably ask her to marry him soon."

Micah shivered. "Just the thought of being tied to that woman for the rest of my life gives me the creeps, but there is love out there for everyone." He clasped Crayson on the shoulder. "See, bruh. If Roxanne found love, there's a chance that your ugly ass will find someone, too."

"Get away from me with that mess." Crayson shrugged off Micah's hand. "Plus, this conversation isn't about me. It's about our porn star brother, Malakai."

"Fuck you," I said, giving him a playful shove. "You should be watching out for Mama since you know as soon as I'm married, she's looking at you next."

"I don't see how you figure that." Crayson took a swig of

his Corona. "Caden still lives in town. She can't pressure me all the way in New York."

"You're the oldest by two minutes," Caden said.

Malik and Micah pinned him with a hard stare. Both were fathers of two, and word was, Mama was still putting on the pressure for them to have more kids.

"Mom is trying to convince Mya and I to adopt," Malik stated. "She said the twins need a sibling."

"And Mom is trying to get us to have another one," Micah said. "But little does she know, Lex is three months pregnant."

My eyes widened as we all looked at Micah. "Congrats, big brother. When do you plan on telling our parents?"

"During family brunch tomorrow," Micah said. "Only Malik and Mya know, and now, you all know. I love that Mom and Dad invite the entire town out for their summer barbeque, but we want to tell our family first."

Wow. I was going to be an uncle ... again. Unable to help myself, I glanced Avery's way and found she was already looking at me. *Damn, I want to kiss her.*

"Do y'all want to head to Joe's for drinks?" Crayson asked. The sun was setting and Joe's was a perfect place to implement the next part of my plan to talk Avery into going on a date with me. A group date wasn't what I had in mind, but it would have to do.

Avery

IT WAS OFFICIAL. I loved the Madden family, especially Malakai's brothers. Separately, they were each amazing in their own way. Together, they were a force to be reckoned with.

"Beautiful sight, isn't it?" Mya, Malik's wife, asked.

"It sure is," I replied, watching Malakai and his brothers catch up with some friends who had entered the bar. I wasn't sure I'd ever seen so many attractive men in one group before. The friends were good looking, but it was those damn brothers who were stealing all of the attention of every woman—and even a few men—in the bar. "I can't believe this small town was breeding men like that."

"Girl, try growing up here." Serenity shook her head. "I was young when their family moved here and opened the B&B, but my two older sisters said that every girl wanted to get a piece of a Madden brother. Just seeing all six of them walk around in town was enough to stop traffic."

"Micah's still sexy as all get out," his wife, Lex, said. "But when I first met him, he was so attractive that I didn't know how to behave. Any awkward thing a woman could do or say, I did or said."

"It was hilarious," Mya said. "I was a lot smoother when I started falling for Malik, but my girl Lex was literally tripping over herself and falling to the ground."

Lex shook her head. "Still so embarrassing."

Mya and Lex were two of the four founders of Elite Events Incorporated, one of the top event planning businesses in the United States. I'd even had the pleasure of attending a few parties they'd thrown in the past for different clients.

"I remember when Micah first brought you here, Lex," Serenity stated. "It was the talk of the entire town that Micah had brought someone home."

"More like tricked me into coming to his hometown." Lex took a sip of her drink. "Water under the bridge."

Feeling eyes on me, I turned toward Malakai's direction and smiled when I found him watching me over his glass as he drank.

"I've never seen Malakai like this," Mya remarked. "I love seeing him fall for someone. Especially someone like you. Lex and I were talking and we can already tell you help keep him on his toes, but you balance one another out."

Sighing, I broke eye contact. "I'm not sure he's falling for me, but I'm damn sure falling for him."

"Oh, he's falling," Lex said. "Or he's already fallen. Like Mya said, we've never seen him like this."

Serenity laughed. "I tried to tell her the same thing. In New York, he acts the same way. He can't take his eyes off her long enough to even acknowledge other people in the room."

"I usually can't take my eyes off him either," I admitted. "I even tried and failed."

"Sounds about right whenever a Madden is concerned," Mya said with a laugh. "Are you feeling him as much as he's feeling you?"

I fidgeted with my napkin. "Yes. Or maybe I'm feeling him more than he is me. I'm not sure."

"Oh, honey, I doubt that," Lex said. "But Crayson did tell us that the whole dating on Twitter thing was your idea."

I sighed. "It was. I don't know what I was thinking."

"You were thinking that hell would have to freeze over before you let yourself fall for him," Mya said. "Am I close to being right?"

"Something like that," I said with a laugh.

"I think you succeeded in the reason you were doing it,"

Serenity explained. "Malakai's image has taken a complete three-sixty, and even though people are eager to see who he will end up with, the sessions with Dr. Walker are giving people a chance to know the real Malakai."

"I don't regret coming up with this idea," I clarified. "But I do wish that I could shut off my mind sometimes when it comes to that man. We haven't even talked about what the heck we're doing or why he invited me to his hometown. What if all I'm feeling is one-sided?"

Mya opened her mouth to speak, but closed it when the men returned to the table nodding their heads to the R&B song that was playing through the speakers.

"Care to dance?" Malik asked Mya. She eagerly nodded her head before placing a sweet kiss on his lips.

"Come on, baby." Micah helped Lex from her seat. "Let's show them the right way to slow dance."

Crayson and Caden took seats on each side of Serenity, leaving Malakai to sit next to me.

"Carter loves this song," Crayson said. My eyes went to Serenity in time to see her slightly cringe. I still didn't know the story, but I remembered Tyler mentioning that they used to date.

"You're an idiot," Caden snapped. "Are you trying to give Serenity a reason to hate the rest of us?"

She gave a forced laugh. "No worries, Caden. Crayson is an idiot whether he's here in Arkansas, in New York, or somewhere else. He doesn't have a cutoff switch."

We all shared a laugh, but my laugh stopped the moment I felt Malakai's lips near my ear. "Dance with me. Please?"

"Sure," I whispered back as I took his outreached hand. Once we reached the dance floor, Malakai chose a spot right in the middle.

Leaning into his arms, we began to sway to the beat of the music was easy. It was looking into his eyes that was almost making me misstep.

"Are you okay?" he asked.

"I'm fine," I lied. "Your family is wonderful. It's just, I was wondering ... I was trying to figure out ... I didn't know if ... Never mind." I closed my mouth.

"Were you trying to ask why I brought you to my hometown?"

"Yes," I said. "Especially when you're dating other women who you could have taken."

"I'm not dating other women," Malakai corrected. "The night after we were together, I called Dr. Parker and told her that although I appreciated all that she'd done, there was only one woman I wanted to date. One woman I woke up every morning thinking about and laid down every night dreaming about."

My eyes widened. "What are you saying?" My heart was beating so fast, I could barely focus on his words.

"Those lunch dates that I went on were me thanking both of the women for dating me during this process, but telling both women that I couldn't continue because I was feeling someone else."

"You mean me?" I asked.

"Yes, you." He laughed. "I brought you to my home-town because I wanted to introduce you to the people I love. I may be a city boy, but I have country roots and if I'm falling for someone and am going to spend a lifetime with that person, I need to see if she can fit in with the town and people who raised me."

Falling for. Love. Lifetime. Keywords from the last few things he'd said floated around my brain as the room around me grew dim so that the only two people who existed where he and I.

"Are you saying you're falling for me?" I asked. I was pretty sure that's exactly what he was saying, but I wanted to be sure.

Instead of responding to me, he leaned his head down and pulled me in for a kiss that was so appetizing, it made my knees buckle. Yet, true to his nature, Malakai was right there by my side, holding me closer to him so that I wouldn't melt to a puddle on the dance floor.

Eventually, my hands made their way around his neck as I pulled him even closer, deepening the kiss. In my Malakai lust fog, I heard a few whistles and catcalls from others in the bar, but I didn't pay them any mind. The only thought on my mind was Malakai's admission that he was falling for me. Now all I had to do was gather my courage to tell him that I was falling for him right back.

SEVENTEEN

Avery

"Do you mind if you have company?"

I glanced up at Mrs. Madden and shook my head. "Not at all. I didn't think anyone else was still up."

"These old bones won't let me sleep sometimes."

I smiled. I'd only gotten to chat with Malakai's parents for a little while, but I'd taken an immediate liking to his mom, Cynthia.

"I see you've already boiled some hot water."

I looked toward the kitchen. "I hope that's okay. I noticed some chamomile tea on the counter and I couldn't sleep."

Cynthia waved her hands. "Don't worry about it, I'm glad you made yourself at home." She poured herself a cup of tea and took a seat across from me at the large dining room table. "We didn't have much time to talk, but I wanted

BLESSED BY MALAKAI   157

to tell you that I'm glad you were able to make the trip to Arkansas."

"I'm glad Malakai invited me." I took a sip of my tea. "Your bed and breakfast is beautiful and so cozy for such a grand space."

"Thanks sweetie. My husband Mason and I work hard at making this a place that feels like family to anyone who may be traveling to our town or for our family who may pay us a visit."

I glanced around at the elegant, yet vintage, décor. "I can fit my entire New York apartment in half of this room."

"I remember when my boys, Malakai and Crayson, were sharing a one bedroom apartment in New York years ago. Mason and I came to visit them and all four of us could barely fit in there."

I laughed. "I can't imagine Malakai and Crayson sharing such a small space."

"They sure did sweetie." Cynthia sipped her tea and got more comfortable in her seat. "I think they rented that place for a couple years together."

"I would have paid good money to see that," I stated.

"It was a sight to see since those two could barely fit in the space, but they made it work like they always do." Cynthia gave a half-smile. "You see, out of all my sons, Malakai and Carter were always the hardest to read. Malakai always viewed life differently than anyone else, which meant, you had to communicate with him differently. While Carter had Caden, Crayson was the one connected with Malakai on a level the others couldn't. Crayson was like his shadow and when Malakai reached a point in his life when we knew times were difficult for him despite the fact that he didn't want us to know what was going on, we found comfort in knowing that Crayson would be there for him."

I couldn't help but smile as I listened to Mrs. Madden reminisce about stories of Malakai when he was younger. "He always seems so comfortable in his own skin," I stated. "Even though I've heard him talk about the struggles he went through to try and find his own place in school and life, in some ways, the artist in him has always seemed to be confident to walk his path."

Cynthia squinted her eyes. "Did you know my son before he hired you to be his image consultant?"

I was sure my face looked flushed as I answered, "Not really, but I've followed his work and I admire him as an artist."

Judging by the look on her face, she wasn't buying my answer, but it was the truth. I hadn't had the pleasure of knowing Malakai before he'd hired me. Of course, I'd known about him through research and being a fan of his work all these years, but I hadn't known the real Malakai. At least, not like I was getting to know him now.

"He's really talented," I continued, taking another sip of my tea. I didn't know why she was making me so nervous, but my anxiousness reached an all-time high when Cynthia asked, "Did you realize you were in love with my son before or after he hired you?"

I spit my tea across the table, grateful that I didn't get any on Mrs. Madden, but embarrassed that her question had caught me so off guard, I'd basically become a human water hose.

I immediately ran to the kitchen to get some paper towels to clean up the mess. "I am so sorry Mrs. Madden. I didn't mean to do that."

In my embarrassed dash to the kitchen, I hadn't noticed that she was laughing with tears streaming out the corner of her eyes.

"Don't worry about it." Cynthia wiped the tears from her eyes. "I take that to mean you were in love with him before he hired you, which is what I predicted. But sweetie, I know you aren't like the consultants he hired previously." She placed her hand over my fidgety one that was still wiping off the contents of my tea. "The reason I asked is because I haven't seen Malakai this happy in years and I know you contributed to calming his state of mind. So thank you for making my son whole again. Mason and I appreciate it more than you'll ever know."

I tried to slow my breathing, but my heart was still beating fast. "Malakai is an amazing man and I've enjoyed getting to know him more. But we ... But I ...—." I sighed, unable to put my words together. "I care for him much more than I should, but the situation is so complicated."

"Then un-complicate it." Cynthia pinned me with her motherly eyes. "Sweetie, you can't fight what's in your heart no more than my son can fight what's in his. We may not have gotten to truly talk until now, but I've been watching you interact with my son and the town since you arrived and I'm very impressed by what I see. You're a special woman Avery."

I smiled. "Thank you for the compliment, Mrs. Madden. It means a lot to me." I refilled my cup of tea before returning to my seat at the table. "I just wish I could see the future sometimes."

"I know sweetie. Don't we all." Cynthia tapped soothing strokes on my hands. Soon, I began to calm down. "But I think I can see you and Malakai's future."

My eyes widened in curiosity. "What do you see?"

I expected Mrs. Madden to say she could see us dating or married. Maybe moving in together. However, the last thing I expected her to say was, "Kids. I see six kids in your future just like Mason and I had, with the first one being born next year."

And just like that, half of my new cup of tea flew from my mouth and landed across the table again.

Malakai

"IS THIS A GOOD IDEA?"

I glanced back at Avery, noting the worried look on her face. "We'll be fine. Don't worry about it. I used to come here all the time as a kid."

Avery looked back at my parent's large barbecue as we ascended up the small hill. "I just don't want anyone to be upset at us for missing any of the festivities."

I shrugged. "I didn't get to see you all morning, so the town can wait." When we reached our destination, I removed large branches that were blocking our path. "Here we are."

Avery squinted her eyes. "And where is here exactly?"

I pointed to the shed. "This shed has been here since my parents brought the place and it also serves as the best hide out on the property because no one ever comes here but me."

I opened the door and pulled Avery inside of the dusty

interior. She coughed as the dust filled the air. "Pretty inter-esting hideout spot."

I laughed as she waved her arms in the air to clear out the dust. Before long, I was coughing too. "Don't worry. I only came in here to get something I'd hidden an hour ago." I grabbed the picnic basket I'd stashed and led us back into the fresh air.

"Did you really pack us a picnic?" Her eyes lit up and I couldn't help but smile at how easily she got excited.

"I did." I opened the basket and pulled out the red blanket that I laid on the grass in front of the shed. After Avery and I were seated, I pulled out two sandwiches and water bottles. "It's not much, but if we get too full my Mom will kill us."

Avery laughed. "Yeah, she would. But this is perfect." We perched our backs against the outside of the shed. "This gives us a bird's eye view of the party."

I nodded. "I used to always sit out here and people watch. It was nice to see what was going on without anyone knowing you were up here."

"I could spend all day on this hill." She took a bite of her sandwich and scooted closer to me. "Did you ever paint up here."

I nodded my head. "You know me too well. I used to spend hours painting here. In a house full of people, it was the only place I could get some real privacy."

"I bet," she said with a laugh. "Since it was only me and Vanny as far as siblings go, I had a lot of my own space because of our age difference."

At the mention of her sister, I wanted to ask if she'd talked to her, but I didn't want to pry. "Must have been nice to have your own space."

"It was." She took a sip of her water. "I meant to tell you that I took your advice and I called Vanny."

"You did? How did it go?"

She smiled. "It went good. I've really missed her and I wasn't sure how much until we FaceTimed. We made a promise to try and talk at least once a month, if not more. And she also told me she's one month pregnant."

"That's great news." I leaned over to give her a quick hug. "I'm glad the conversation went well and I'm glad she's expecting. You mentioned that she really wanted to have kids."

"I'm happy for them. Vanny deserves this and I can put my differences aside to re-build my relationship with her and to have a relationship with my niece."

When her eyes looked away from the party and met mines, I held her gaze. "I'm proud of you."

"Thanks." She studied my eyes. "Every time you look at me like this, I have to remember to breath."

I smiled. "That's funny because every time I look at you like this, I forget whatever it is we're talking about."

She laughed. "I'm sure you say that to all the ladies."

My face grew serious. "Not all. Just one." I placed my right hand on her cheek as our faces inched closer together.

"Your eyes evoke the same feelings in me as your paintings," she whispered. "Each brush stroke evokes emotion. Every color seems to have been handpicked to dance on the canvas."

Damn, that mouth. Every time she talked about my work, she did so in such a poetic way, that it made me speechless. "Avery, I could paint you a thousand times and never be able to capture the raw makeup of your beauty and character. You talk about how my art inspires you." My eyes dropped to her lips. "But it's you who inspires me."

I kissed the smile off her lips as we forgot about the sandwiches and indulged in a kiss that left me wishing we were somewhere more private where I could do what I really wanted to do to her. *Patience, Madden. You need to have patience.* I had a surprise for Avery that I couldn't wait to share with her, but it would have to wait until tomorrow. As badly as I wanted to strip her naked on this blanket, Avery was worth the wait. *She'll always be worth the wait.*

EIGHTEEN

Avery

"Where are you taking me?" I asked as I glanced around the abandoned warehouse. When Malakai had knocked on my door in the wee hours of the morning and asked me to join him for a short drive before brunch, I hadn't known that a short drive actually meant an hour-long drive outside of town.

"You do realize that dragging me to an abandoned warehouse in the middle of nowhere is really creepy, right? Especially after you dragged me to an empty shed yesterday morning."

"Stop overreacting." He unlocked a door that led to a stairwell. Walking up the stairs, I didn't even try to hide my appreciation for the way his ass looked his jeans or the way his broad shoulders stretched under the simple white tee he was wearing.

"I'm not used to seeing you dress this casual, but I like it," I said.

"Thank you." He glanced back to look at me. "You're looking mighty good in those blue jean shorts and pink tee. Almost didn't make it out of your room when I got you after you'd gotten dressed."

I lightly swatted at his back. "You're such a flirt."

"You bring it out of me." When we reached the top of the stairs, he pulled out his keys.

"How do you have keys to this warehouse? Isn't it abandoned?"

"Not exactly," he replied, unlocking another door. "I own this building."

"Really? Then why does it look like no one owns it? Did you just get it?"

"I bought it a few years ago, but I'm not sure what I want to do with the lower level yet. I bought it for this top level." He opened the door, revealing a gorgeous loft that rivaled the beauty of the one he had back in New York.

"This is amazing." Spinning around, I took in all of the artwork and exposed wood and pipes throughout the place.

He turned on a few standing fans that were in the living area. "I used to come here back in the day with some friends from high school when it was an old candy factory. The factory shut down years ago, but the owner hadn't wanted to sell. When the owner passed away three years ago, his son sold it to me. I pay a local boy in town to check on the area every other week and clean up. Caden has him check on a property he has a mile down the road, too. If I give him notice, he even makes sure the fridge is stocked when I get to town."

I walked past the kitchen and into one of the sectioned

off rooms. A lot of the pieces in the room seemed similar to pieces that I'd seen in his gallery. Different since Malakai never painted the same piece, but still within the same realm of his other work.

Walking across the hall to the other room revealed more art pieces and a few sculptures. "Did you have these walls added to the loft for privacy?"

"No, it was like that when I brought the place," Malakai yelled from the front room. "The previous owners used to rent this space out from time to time. I did some renovating, but I tried to keep a lot of the loft authentic to what it was before."

"Great choice." Stepping over the white tarp covering the floor, I walked over to the huge king bed in the corner of the room. Right above the bed was a beautiful oil painting with rich, cool colors. Yet, it wasn't the painting that made me pause. It was the words underneath the painting that made me hold my breath. For what reason, I wasn't sure. I was still trying to figure it out why when Malakai came to stand inside of the door entrance.

"That oil painting is similar to one of the first pieces I ever sold for a large sum of money," he said. "I honestly wouldn't even have made the sale if it hadn't been for my ex-girlfriend who'd convinced me to sneak into this ritzy art gallery party in New York one day. I guess you could say, she jump-started my hustle."

I smiled. "Sounds like she helped you out quite a bit."

"She did." He glanced up at the oil painting. "When we'd first met, she was in a bad relationship, but she and I would often frequent the corner store in Harlem. One day, we got to talking and then every week for about three months, we would meet and talk about anything we wanted.

Life. Our careers. I was a starving artist and she was an aspiring singer, so we both were trying to make it.

"I remember the day she told me she'd left her ex and wanted to be with me being one filled with excitement and happiness. She knew I was interested in her and for me, she was one of the first people who truly believed that I could be the Malakai Madden I am today besides my close family."

"She sounds pretty great," I said, studying the sadness in his eyes. "How long were you together?"

"I was with her for almost four years. It was in the third year that her ex started back contacting her and popping up everywhere we were. He said he was a changed man and he wanted her back. I remember Crayson coming down to New York when he was thinking about moving here too and me introducing them. He said he liked her, but after staying with us for a week, he was worried she was going to hurt me because she still seemed hung up on her ex. A few months after they'd met, I came home one day and all of her stuff was gone. She'd completely moved out with nothing more than a letter saying she was still in love with her ex and had gotten back with him. She thanked me for the past few years."

I blew out a breath.

"Can you believe that? All that time we'd spent together and the only thing she could do was tell me thanks, not I'm sorry for breaking your heart. Just thanks."

Stepping closer to him, I placed my hand on his cheek. "I'm sorry you had to go through that. I know what it feels like to be cheated on."

"I was pissed for a long time," he said. "They married a few months after she left me and I only found out because she'd told the owner of that café we used to go to who told me. To this day, Crayson is the only one who knows about her. For a year, I didn't hear anything from her, and then out of the blue, she contacts me and tells me that she is in trouble and that her husband is mentally and physically abusing her."

My hand flew to my mouth. "That's so horrible. Did she leave him?"

"She didn't," he said. "She tried to, but he always found her." His eyes went back to the oil painting on the wall. "Crayson had finally moved to New York, and I was headed to my first art gallery release that was featuring one of my pieces when she called me for help. She'd been calling me for months, but every time I would show up, her ex would be there and she'd claim that everything was fine. I missed a lot of opportunities dropping everything for her, just for her to claim she didn't need me. I had to get my life back and I needed to let her go."

I could barely take the sadness in his eyes, and even before he got the words out, I knew I wouldn't like how this story ended.

"I choose the wrong night to decide to let shit go." He ran his fingers across his face. "The police called me the next morning because I was the last call she'd made before her husband banged her head against their bathroom tub after an altercation. Neighbors say they heard a lot of yelling and screaming before everything went silent and her husband ran out the front door. He left her to bleed out instead of calling 9 1 1, and by the time one of the neighbors called, it was too late. They picked him up at a motel that night."

His story was heart-wrenching and I hadn't even known I'd began crying while he spoke until he was wiping away my tears.

"What was her name?" I asked, realizing he'd never said it.

"Nevaeh," he replied, blinking a few times. "I haven't said her name since she was killed."

I studied his eyes. "How does it feel to say it?"

He seemed to think about it for a few moments before answering, "Relieved. Like a weight I hadn't known I'd been holding lifted."

"You needed to say her name." Leaning forward, I rested my forehead against his. "No matter how tragic the relationship ended, Neveah will always be a part of what made you the man you are today. Lord knows I don't like everything that has happened to me in the past, but if we could only remember all of the good things and forgot the bad, we wouldn't recognize what we fight so hard for or remember the lessons we've learned along the way."

He kissed my forehead before leaning back to stare into my eyes. "You're not like most women."

"Makes us even since you aren't like most men." I was about to kiss him when a few more missing pieces to a puzzle I didn't even know I was putting together began to fall into place.

"Neveah," I said. "Neveah ... That's Heaven spelled backward. The sculpture that's in your gallery that you've never explained why you created it to anyone, that's supposed to be Neveah, right? You created it as a way to remember her?"

His eyes widened. "I can't believe you put that together."

I wrapped my arms around his waist. "The sculpture is even more beautiful now that I know she was the inspiration behind it."

"She wasn't the only person who's inspired me," he said,

his voice growing huskier. He glanced up at the wall and read the quote. "When you accept that things will happen that you cannot change, you can enjoy life and appreciate its beauty."

He gazed down at me. "I was in a dark place after Neveah died, and the last thing I wanted to do was paint or create. Crayson tried his best to get me out of my funk, but nothing worked. I was tired of participating in art competitions like I had in the past, but decided to participate in a few more after Crayson convinced me to get out of New York and clear my head. As you mentioned a few weeks ago, I lost the first five, including Memphis, but I was on fire after that."

My breathing grew scattered as I studied the look in his eyes, unable to decipher what he was thinking, but feeling anxious for some reason.

"During the competitions, the audience was asked not to speak so that they wouldn't interfere with the artists' creativity. I remember standing there, glancing at what the other artists were doing, then looking back to my blank canvas, regretting that I'd signed up to compete. I felt like I'd lost my edge. I'd lost my way. Then, I looked out into the audience and saw a woman in a big, floppy hat and sunglasses, who was holding up a sign that said—"

"When you accept that things will happen that you cannot change, you can enjoy life and appreciate its beauty." My hand flew to my mouth. "I was in Memphis for a bachelorette party for one of my friends, but I only agreed to attend her trip because I'd heard that you would be there. It was so hot that day and the sun was beaming, so I borrowed one of the girl's hats."

"I knew it was you." His lips curled to the side in a smile. "The minute you told me that you were at my

Memphis competition back when we were at my gallery, I knew it had to be you."

"You should have won that day," I said. "You may not have been able to finish, but your half-done painting was better than all of the others full work."

"I was fine with losing that one." His eyes grew serious. "Avery, you may not have realized this at the time, but I'm telling you now, you were the reason I was able to continue painting in the on-the-road competition. I didn't know. Couldn't even tell how you looked with the glasses and floppy hat. I was in a bad place back then and the heat hadn't made it better. Then I read your words, and something just clicked. Your words hit me right in the chest, which was exactly where I needed to be resuscitated."

His eyes dropped to my necklace. "Just like now, you were wearing a necklace with a feather on it. I went to find you after the competition, but you'd disappeared. I'd almost thought I'd dreamed you up, until that night in my gallery."

I can't believe this ... "I knew the quote sounded familiar, but I couldn't place it since I wasn't thinking about it as something I said. Honestly, I forgot that I'd even wrote those words on a piece of paper and held it up for you. I didn't even know you'd seen it."

"I'd seen it," he said. "I saw you that day even if I couldn't make out your face." His eyes dipped back to my mouth. "I see you now, Avery."

I should have been prepared for how different this kiss would feel, but I wasn't. Not at all. The feel of his lips on mine was even more intoxicating than our previous kisses had been. Malakai wasted no time lifting my bra and shirt over my head before removing his shirt. He removed my jeans and panties with the same skill, but when he reached his own jeans, I had other plans.

My hands unbuttoned him, removing his jeans and boxers with a delicacy I didn't think I could find given how badly I wanted to rip the damn things off. The bed was only a few feet away, but I found myself sliding down to the floor over the white tarp that was lying there.

Once I had him naked, I eagerly opened my mouth to slip his long, thick dick into my mouth. The groan he released as I began moving my tongue in a rhythm that I hoped would give him pleasure encouraged me to relax my throat muscles even more and suck him even deeper.

"Oh, fuck," he said, lightly gripping the back of my head. Increasing my strokes, I took him even deeper, swirling my tongue in a way that made my jaw sore, but I didn't care. I wanted him to release himself. I wanted to hear him groan even louder as I pushed him to the brink and brought him over the edge.

Granting my wish, his warning that he was close came out as a groan right before he released an orgasm so hard, it had him convulsing in his standing position. Working my mouth over time, I sucked in every last drop of his salty taste, surprising myself by the fact that I didn't spill any.

I expected him to need a moment to gather himself, but instead, he got on his knees and was licking me into a toe-curling orgasm quicker than I could process. In the back of my mind, I briefly thought about the fact that Malakai had given me more orgasms than I could count, which was saying a lot for a woman who'd never experienced orgasms previous to him.

I must have still been in a lustful daze, because I didn't notice Malakai putting on protection and entering me until he was already halfway inside. I cried out in pleasure as he began moving, only momentarily glancing around when I felt a wave of wetness flow through our bodies.

Glancing down, I noticed he'd knocked over two buckets of paint, Malakai's strokes causing us to get the blue and green paint everywhere.

"This tarp may have to go on a wall," Malakai said, his eyes sparkling with interest as he took a moment to glance around our body at the wonderful shapes we were making.

When he switched our position and let me get on top, I could see the beautiful creation we were making as our bodies used the paint in a way I'd never imagined before. I could already make out my butt print and would have focused more on the other shapes and designs had Malakai not changed our angle so that I was still on top, but tilted forward, giving him a better angle.

I opened my mouth to groan, or moan, yell his name. Hell, I wasn't even sure because what came out was more of a screeching noise as my orgasm seemed to come out of nowhere and smack me across the face. Malakai followed soon after, his noises matching mine, only on a more masculine level.

Ten minutes later, the paint was starting to dry a little, yet we still lay there, naked and intertwined in each other.

"Remember when I said I'm falling for you?" Malakai asked.

"Of course," I replied, kissing the bottom of his chin. "I'd never forget that."

"Good." He leaned up on one elbow so that he was staring into my eyes in that intense way he always did. "Then I guess it's only fair to let you know that I wasn't being honest earlier."

I studied his eyes for regret. "What do you mean?"

He gently touched my chin as he leaned closer to me. "What I should have told you was that I'm way past falling,

Avery. I've fallen. I'm already in love more than I have been with anyone in my entire life."

I was sure the smile that crossed my face looked like one of those Chuck-E-Cheese grins. "I love you, too." I glanced at his lips. "I've loved you for a while now, so I guess you're in good company."

I placed a kiss on his lips that was supposed to be quick, but escalated into one that had me moaning in his mouth, ready for the next wrong. If his phone hadn't started ringing for the second time, we would have continued kissing.

"Hello?" He laughed. "Damn. Okay, bruh. Tell her we're on our way."

"Is everything okay?" I asked him after he'd hung up the phone.

"Everything's fine, it's just Cynthia Madden making her demands per usual." Rising, he reached for me and helped me stand. "We should get back for brunch. My mom wants to show off the woman who's stolen her son's heart, so it's officially not just an immediate family festivity anymore. Apparently, anyone in the town who didn't meet you the past couple days wants to officially meet you before we fly back."

I laughed. "I'm fine with that. Everyone I met yesterday was great and I love meeting new people."

Malakai froze. "Clearly, you don't know how clingy the residents of Cranberry Heights are. Just like the internet, they have no chill. By the time we leave tomorrow, they all will have programmed their number in your phone. Hell, they may have already talked Serenity into giving it to them already."

As if on cue, my phone began ringing with a number I didn't know. After a while, I answered a few of them, but Malakai was right. The Cranberry Heights folks had no chill. It didn't matter to me though because I would take a hundred more phone calls for a man like Malakai Madden. On the car ride back, he asked me if I'd finally go on an official date with him. Of course I agreed, on one condition ... No cameras. No Twitter. No live videos.

EPILOGUE

Five months later ...

Malakai

"BRUH, why are you still watching Avery every time she moves around the room? You already got the chick. Worried she really doesn't want your ass?"

Malik popped Crayson on the shoulder. "Quit teasing him. Proposing is nerve-wracking enough without feedback from the peanut gallery."

"Y'all teased me," Micah said. "It's Malakai's turn. He can take it."

Nothing was getting to me tonight. Not even Crayson's antics. Avery was standing with my sisters-in-law and looked breathtaking in her sleek black dress and red pumps. Her curls were luscious and wild just the way I loved them, and she was sporting her black-rimmed glasses that I'd learned she only wore for reading. I'd asked her to wear them more often because I loved that sexy librarian vibe she gave off in them. Tonight, she'd even chosen to wear red lipstick that was making my dick jump in anticipation of what the night would bring.

Walking over to me, Caden placed his hand on my shoulder. "She'll say yes. That woman loves you too much to say no."

I glanced at my watch and noticed I had twenty minutes to show time. I knew Caden was right. I wouldn't be proposing to Avery if I didn't think she was ready. However, it didn't make me any less nervous.

Most people dated years before they got engaged, but we had only been together officially for five months even though I'd known her for longer. When we'd gotten back to New York after my parents' summer party, I took Avery on a date every day for two weeks straight before we got into a normal dating pattern. I thought she'd call me crazy for taking up her nights every day, but we'd only grown closer and as promised, I'd finished my live sessions with Dr. Walker, ending my last session by saying I'd found the woman of my dreams and was officially off the market.

Avery hadn't wanted to say I was off the market because that would imply that I was in an engagement when I wasn't. I told her that the minute I realized she was my future, I was off the market. I laughed it off, but I'd been dead serious. When a Madden man committed, he committed for life. Point blank, period.

"Why the hell did you choose to propose on Christmas Eve in New York?" Crayson asked. "You could have chosen someplace warm and had our family and hers meet you there instead."

Avery had expected my parents to attend my holiday gallery show to reveal my latest piece that consisted of a painting that spanned over twelve canvases that positioned together fit into a floor to ceiling work of art. I'd never done a twelve-foot piece, but I was so proud of how this piece had turned out.

"It's my proposal, so I'm doing things my way," I said to my brother. "If someone is ever crazy enough to marry you, then you can do things your way."

"It will be on a beach, or someplace warm," Crayson stated. "Y'all can quote me on that shit."

My brothers shook their heads. Minutes later, Serenity nodded her head to me and then Tyler, giving us the cue that it was time to make our move before she made the announcement to the audience to head toward the right side of the gallery that had been closed off until the reveal.

"Okay, fellas. It's show time."

My brothers followed me into the hallway right outside of the door that led to the section of the new artwork. Fifteen minutes ago, I'd escorted my parents back there when Avery's parents and sister had arrived. Dr. Walker, Dr. Parker, Steve the cameraman, and Director Ben were all in attendance for Steve to capture what I hoped would be my last Twitter live video ever.

"Are you ready, son?" my mom asked as soon as I reached the group.

"Of course he's ready, Cynthia," my dad, Mason, said. "Don't hover over the boy."

I gave my mom a kiss on the cheek before hugging my dad and doing the same to Avery's parents and sister.

"It's time, folks. Follow me." The short walk down the hallway to the side door by my new artwork seemed to take a lot longer than I'd ever remembered it taking before.

"Proud of you, bruh," Crayson said.

"Leave it all out there," Caden added.

"You got this," Malik whispered as we neared the door.

"And just think," Micah said lowly, "had crazy Roxanne not blasted your business on Twitter then had a herd of women chasing you all through Chicago, you may not have found the woman of your dreams."

My laugh was loud, but I'd needed it to loosen up a bit. Micah was right. It was hard to imagine myself running from a herd of women, although I'd been there, so I knew it had really happened.

I just wasn't the same man that I once was and I couldn't go another day without proposing to Avery. I led everyone in front of the collection of canvases that were covered by a large white tarp. Steve set up his camera in the perfect place and Tyler came from around the corner, signaling that Serenity had made her announcement.

People began filing into the space pretty quickly, but my eyes stayed glued to Avery's. The moment her eyes landed on her parents and sister, she froze and her hands flew to her face. Tyler gently grabbed her arm and led her the rest of the way to me, handing me the mic like we'd planned.

"First, I want to thank everyone for coming," I said to the audience. "Although many of you are gathered here tonight for the reveal of my latest work, I wanted to touch on another topic first." I held Avery's hand in mine to try and ease her nerves since she still seemed to be in shock.

"Some of you may remember the series of live Twitter sessions that I did with Dr. Walker, guest starring Dr. Parker, this past summer. Well, after I finished taping, I received a lot of inquiries regarding the woman who'd stolen the heart of Malakai Madden. At the time, I didn't want to announce it to the world when I hadn't told her in person yet. You see, Avery was my image consultant and the brains behind 'Malakai Madden's Journey to Love'. However, what she didn't know was that while she was busy working with Dr. Walker and Dr. Parker to create the perfect plan, I was falling hard for her. I'm sure you noticed that my last three sessions didn't show any highlights from actual dates." I glanced at Avery. "That's because Avery Nightingale had stolen my heart."

A round of *aww's*, filled the crowd. "But little did Avery know, even when we didn't realize it, our time together was being documented." I nodded to Tyler and Steve to begin playing the video we'd created. Avery's mouth dropped when she noticed one of the first scenes was when she'd interviewed. Music was over the words, but the look of interest on my face and hers was clear.

The next scene was when Avery had arrived during my first live video. For this part, you could hear my voice as I discussed what I was looking for while staring solely at Avery. I laughed when I heard a few people in the audience say they were wondering what I had been looking at.

The videos continued with ones of us in the bar, ones of us in Cranberry Heights, some others from dates we'd taken recently. When Tyler and Serenity had initially shown me the videos they had been taking, I'd been caught off guard. Then Tyler showed me a few that had been posted by folks in my hometown and I realized that people genuinely wanted me to find love and wanted to know if Avery was the one.

After the video ended, Avery's eyes were watery with unshed tears.

"Avery, what you saw in that video was only a token of the memorable times we've shared together, and although I know we hadn't planned to fall for one another, I think fate had other plans."

I pulled out the black velvet ring box, and knelt on one

knee. "Avery Nightingale, contrary to what Twitterland may like to believe, meeting you is what has been my best blessing." The audience laughed since that #BlessedBy-Malakai hashtag was still trending despite my best efforts. At least now, it was trending for my artwork from clients or when someone brought or shared one of my pieces and not my skills in the bedroom. "Will you complete my journey and marry me?"

"Yes," she said, wiping away a few tears. "Of course I will." She squealed when I placed the diamond ring on her finger, and as beautiful as the ring was, my mind was only on tasting her sweet lips again.

"I love you, Malakai," she said in between kisses.

I broke the kiss to look her in the eyes. "I love you, too, baby." Glancing around, I made sure no one could hear what I was about to say. "I have another surprise for you when we get home."

Her eyes widened. "Is it my painting? You finally finished it?"

I nodded. A month ago, Avery had done the honor of posing nude for me since I was dying to capture her beauty and essence.

"I hope you made me look good," she teased.

I smiled slyly. "You already know I did. But if you don't like it, you can pose for me again."

She playfully swatted me on my arm, but I was being serious. I'd paint her every day if she'd let me. Avery wasn't just my inspiration ... She was my truth. She was my future. She was my everything.

THE END

WOULD LOVE TO HEAR FROM YOU!

I hope you enjoyed #BlessedByMalakai! I love to hear from readers! Thanks in advance for any reviews, messages or emails :). Keep turning for more goodies!

Also, stop by my online Coffee Corner and get the latest info on my books, contests, events and more!

www.bit.ly/SherelleGreensCoffeeCorner

Want exclusive content? Join my newsletter to learn more:

https://sherellegreen.com/newsletter/

Save and Author! Leave a Review!

ONCE UPON A BRIDESMAID SERIES

When four bridesmaids come together to support their best friend's wedding, they realize that most of the people they know have already tied the knot. Whether unlucky in love or single by choice, these besties make a pact to change their relationship status. The goal is simple... Each woman has one year to find Mr. Right and say 'I do'. Between passionate one-night-stands and best friend hookups, these bridesmaids are in for a wild ride. Are they in over their heads? Or will one impulsive wedding pact change their lives... forever.

Yours Forever excerpt on next page

Yours Forever by Sherelle Green (Book 1)

Beyond Forever by Elle Wright (Book 2)

Embracing Forever by Sheryl Lister (Book 3)

Hopelessly Forever by Angela Seals (Book 4)

EXCERPT: YOURS FOREVER

The Pact

There are two things in life that a woman always needs to have in her possession: her sanity and her punani. Grandma Pearl's words echoed in Mackenzie Cannon's mind as she fidgeted in her cushioned wicker chair and ignored the conversation taking place between her best friends.

Grandma Pearl had always been one of Mac's favorite people. Not only had she been a classy woman with her large church hats and beautiful thick figure, but she'd also been the one to teach Mac the art of talking dirty without it sounding dirty.

Granted, there were times that Mac would rather say *pussy* instead of *punani*, but she kept it as classy as she could.

"I bet he tastes as good as he looks," Mac said aloud, taking in the delicious sight of the best man in a tux. "Can someone please get me a glass of water?"

When he turned to look her way, she didn't even try to hide her thorough perusal of his body. Now that one of her best friends was married and dancing with her new husband on the dance floor, Mac could loosen her bridesmaid dress and focus on the tall cup of coffee who'd held her attention all weekend long.

"Seriously, Mac! Are you even listening to what I'm saying?"

Mac turned to face her best friend since childhood, Quinn Jacobs. They may be polar opposites, but Mac had a soft spot for Q. Despite their differences, they were extremely close. "I heard you, Q. I agree, Ava and Owen look happy. But in case you didn't notice, I'm trying my best focus on something a little more interesting than the newlyweds."

Mac, Quinn, Raven Emerson, and Ryleigh Fields had grown up in the small town of Rosewood Heights, South Carolina and had been friends since they were little girls. Although they each decided to pursue careers in other states, the women had returned to their hometown to celebrate the union of the fifth member of their pack—and the only friend still residing in Rosewood—Ava Prescott, to her husband, Owen Sullivan. The beautiful wedding had taken place in Rosewood Estates, a staple in the small lake town and perfect for a woman who valued tradition and community like Ava did.

"Why must you be so rude?" Raven asked, shaking her head. "You know how Q gets when she's talking about romance."

"Ha!" Mac said with a laugh. "Anyone within a thirty-mile radius can hear her squeal when she starts talking about love and shit."

"Girl, you can say that again," Ryleigh said, giving Mac a high-five. It was normal for Ryleigh and Mac to agree. Both were headstrong and loved cozying up to a good-looking man every once and a while. At their high school dances, they'd often place bets on who could get the most numbers. Typically, they both took turns winning.

Quinn cleared her throat. "If everyone's done making fun of me, can we please continue the discussion?"

Mac turned her body in her chair so that she could face each of the women just as the waiter approached to take their drink order.

"I'll have another mojito," Mac said as she polished off her third glass in preparation for her fourth. When it came to getting through weddings, Mac had a firm drinking rule... More booze equaled more fun.

Conversation flowed between the friends as if it hadn't been a while since they'd last seen each other. Living in different states meant a lot of emails, calls, and text messages passed between them. Despite the different area codes, they made an effort to have a group conference call at least once a month to stay in touch.

The young waiter returned with their drinks and shot her what she assumed was his killer smile. Mac barely paid the youngin' any mind.

"I think we should toast," Quinn said, lifting her margarita high. "Here's to us all finding that special someone and saying 'I do' by this time next year."

Raven froze, her glass in mid-air. "Are you *crazy*?"

"Oh hell no," Ryleigh said at the same time, almost spilling her drink when she placed her glass on the table.

Mac was shaking her head in disagreement before Quinn even got out the last word. "The only thing I'm saying 'I do' to is one night with that tall, mouth-watering best man standing over there." She glanced over her shoulder in his direction.

Quinn placed her glass down and perked up in her

chair. "Oh, come on you guys! We're twenty-nine years old! I don't want to be pushing a stroller when I'm fifty."

"If Janet Jackson can do it, so can we," Mac said with a smile.

"I'm being serious." Quinn scooted forward in her chair. "Think about it. Just about everybody we know has gotten married in the last three years, yet we're all still single. Wouldn't it be nice to have a warm, hard body to snuggle up to every night? To not have to worry about those awkward bar or club meetings? I mean, how hard could it be?" She lifted her glass again. "Come on! We can do this. Right here. Right now. Let's make a pact. Better yet, let's make this a best friend challenge."

Mac winced. *Damn, Q just said the magic words.* They were known to place a wager on anything and Mac *hated* to lose. Mac watched Raven slowly lift her glass to Quinn's. A quick glance at Ryleigh proved that she shared the same sentiment as Mac, but she slowly began to lift her glass as well.

"Oh shit," Mac huffed. "Are you seriously trying to make us all agree to be married before this time next year?"

Quinn smirked. "I thought the *Queen of Friends with Benefits* wasn't afraid of anything."

Mac rolled her eyes at the not-so-endearing nickname her friends had given her back when they were in high school. "I'm not afraid of anything."

"Then raise your glass, girlfriend," Quinn teased.

Mac hesitantly bit her bottom lip before finally raising her glass.

"To finding that special someone and saying 'I do' by this time next year," Quinn repeated when all four glasses were raised.

Mac felt like she was on auto-pilot as they clinked

glasses before taking a sip of their drinks. *Screw it,* she thought as she downed her entire drink after a few more seconds. There weren't too many things that left Mac speechless, but agreeing to this pact was one for the books. *I definitely need a distraction now*, she thought as her eyes drifted back to the best man.

Mac stood from her chair. "Well, ladies, as fun as this is, I'll have to catch you in the morning for breakfast."

Quinn shook her head. "You won't find your husband by getting in the best man's pants."

Mac smoothed out her bridesmaid dress. "Sweetie, I'm sure my future husband, whomever he may be, will appreciate my sex drive. In the meantime, there are other men who will appreciate it just as much."

Was Mac ashamed that she enjoyed sex so much? Absolutely not. Would Mac ever apologize for having a frivolous fling? No way! She knew who she was and she didn't have to explain herself to anybody.

Quinn shook her head. "It's not always about sex, Mac."

"And marriage isn't always about love and romance." With a wink, Mac made her way across the room, leaving her friends to discuss how shocked they were that she'd agreed to the pact. They were probably assuming she would back out, but there was no way Mac was backing down from a best friend challenge. No way at all.

***

"Beware, my brother. You may have been tempted before, but temptation never looked like that."

Alexander Carter followed his brother's gaze, only to find the sexy bridesmaid that he'd been avoiding all weekend walking toward them. *Damn.* It was almost like she'd been plucked from every fantasy he'd ever had of the opposite sex. Her thick honey-brown curls were pulled to the side, cascading over her shoulders. Alex had always had a thing for big, natural curls and hers were no exception. His fingers itched to run through her hair.

If that wasn't enough to send his libido into overdrive, the woman had enough curves to keep a man occupied for decades. While some men always went after the skinny-model type, Alex preferred a woman with a little more meat on her bones. *And damned if she isn't stacked in all the right places.*

He cleared his throat before leaning against the bar and looking back at his younger brother, Shane. "Yeah, I'm in trouble."

"I told you, big bruh, you were in trouble the minute we went to Ava and Owen's luncheon a couple of days ago. When Owen asked us to be in the wedding last year, he warned you that Ava had some fine-ass friends."

"Yeah, but I didn't think he meant any of them were my type."

Shane laughed. "You know Owen has always been into talking in riddles and shit. He was trying to warn you without saying those exact words."

Alex shook his head. "I've been celibate for two years and haven't given into temptation. There's no way I'm giving in now."

Shane's voice lowered. "Listen, I know the face of a woman on a mission, so you have to ask yourself one question. Can you handle denying yourself a night with a sexy siren like her?"

"Yes, I can."

Shane could barely conceal his grin. "Then good luck, my brother." He glanced over Alex's shoulder. "You're gonna need it."

Shane had only been gone two seconds when she approached. "Hello, mind if I join you?"

Alex turned to face the stunning brown beauty he'd just been speaking about. *Tell her no. Send her on her way. You may have had the strength to avoid women before, but not a woman like her.*

"Sure, please do." Her thigh grazed his as she leaned next to him against the bar. Alex briefly shut his eyes. *Wrong move, my dude.*

"So, what is Alexander Carter's drink of choice?"

He took a sip of his once-forgotten drink. "Cognac on the rocks."

She squinted her eyes. "Smooth, strong, dark. At first it appears simple, but then you take one sip and experience the added element of charm and power." She looked him up and down. "I can see why you like it. It suits you."

Alex grinned slyly. "And what does Miss Mackenzie Cannon drink?"

"Today, mojitos were my drink of choice. But, usually, I'm a White Russian kind of woman."

Alex leaned slightly forward. "A White Russian... Sweet, yet robust. Creamy. The type of drink that sneaks up on you." He observed her a little closer. "And the coffee gives the drink a hint of the unexpected and plays with your taste buds."

When her eyes briefly danced with amusement, Alex noticed they were the color of sweet honey. He licked his lips and her eyes followed the movement.

"Very intuitive, Mr. Carter," Mac said as she stepped a little closer. "I'm not the type of woman to beat around the bush, so I must warn you that I came over here to try and seduce you."

Alex swallowed. "Well, I must say that you're doing a damn good job."

"Oh, I don't know about that, Mr. Carter." She pushed a few of her curls over her shoulder and placed one hand on her hip. "Although I came over here to do the seducing, you're seducing me in ways that you probably don't even realize."

Man, she needs to stop calling me Mr. Carter. Her voice was sultry and as smooth as velvet. Addressing him so formally was only making his pants tighter in the crotch area.

"Want to take a walk?" Mac asked.

If you leave the confides of this reception, you may not be able to control yourself. "Sure," he responded, ignoring the warning.

It was a beautiful September day in Rosewood Heights and Alex found the laid-back lake town extremely relaxing for a city boy like himself.

"I never thought I'd say this, but I miss this small town." Alex glanced at Mac just as she waved to a store owner across the street.

"I can understand why you miss it. I moved around so much as a kid that I don't really have roots anywhere. At least I didn't until I became an adult and settled down on the east coast."

"I know the feeling," Mac said with a laugh. "My family moved around a lot when I was younger, but for some reason, we always came back to Rosewood. And every time we returned, my girlfriends welcomed me back with open arms."

Alex smiled. He hadn't known Mac for more than forty-eight hours, but he'd pegged her as the type that didn't open up easily. The fact that she'd even told him that much surprised him.

They fell into easy conversation with an underline of flirtation in every word they said to one another. As much as Alex missed having sex, he missed the act of flirting even more. In his experience, flirting with a woman meant it would lead to other things. Things of the sexual nature. Things that wouldn't end well for a guy who'd made a vow of celibacy.

"I've done a lot of traveling, but this is still one of my favorite spots," Mac said as they approached a small garden with locks all along the fence. "We call this Love's Last Garden. It's been said that Rosewood Heights is the place where people come to relax and find love. Most of it is a myth, but this was the last garden that was built in the town and many townsfolk fell in love in this very place. Once you find love, you place a lock on the fence."

Alex looked around at the lush greenery and locks positioned about the fence. He couldn't quite place his finger on it, but he felt even more connected with Mac being in this garden. When he turned back to Mac, his eyes met hers. Watching him. Observing him. She bit her lip again in the same way he'd seen her do all day before her eyes dropped to his lips. *What is it with this woman?* He barely knew her, yet something about her drew him in. And without dwelling on his next move, he took two short strides toward her and pulled her to him.

He gave her a few seconds to protest, but when she looked up at him expectantly, he brought his lips down to hers. Alex had meant for it to be a simple kiss, but he should have known that Mac would awaken a desire deep within him, especially after the tension between them all weekend.

She slowly opened her mouth and he took the invitation to add his tongue to the foreplay.

Kissing Mac wasn't what he'd expected. It was so much more. He may be celibate, but he'd had his fair share of kisses. With Mac, she kissed with her entire body, nipping and suckling in a way that was mentally breaking down the walls he usually had up. When her moan drifted to his ears, Alex pulled her even closer, tilting her head for better access. His hands eventually found their way to her ass, cupping her through the material of her dress. Although the sun had set, they kissed in a way that made Alex forget that they were standing in a public garden.

At her next moan, Alex stepped back. *Man, you need to get a grip.* Even with the space between them, he could still feel her heat. If she kissed like that, he could only imagine how she'd be in bed.

They stood there for a couple of minutes, neither saying anything as they took in their fill of one another. Being the CEO of an environmental engineer firm, Alex knew a thing or two about self-control to reach the ultimate goal. He was one of the most controlled people he knew. However, as he got lost in Mac's honey gaze, he couldn't remember the reasons why he'd decided to be celibate in the first place. *Surely there were a list of reasons, right?*

Mac stepped back to him and ran her fingers over his loosened navy blue tie. "Your room or mine?"

This was it. This was the situation he'd been trying to avoid since he'd laid eyes on Mackenzie Carter. The old Alex wouldn't have hesitated to drag Mac to his hotel room and explore her delicious body. However, the new and improved Alex didn't think it was such a good idea. His right and wrong consciousness battled with one another, each arguing their point of view, trying to convince him to take their side. *This should be an easy decision. Say no, remain celibate, and send Mac on her merry way.*

"What will it be, Mr. Carter?" She brought her plump lips to his ear. "Do you want to share a night of unrestrained bliss with yours truly?" She tugged his earlobe between her teeth before soothing the bite with a kiss.

What. The. Fuck. If there was a book on seduction, Mac must have invented it. When she boldly ran her hips over his mid-section, he lost all train of thought. His eyes landed on hers and held her gaze.

"Mine," he said in a firm voice. "It's time that I show you what calling me 'Mr. Carter' does to me."

He didn't even give her a chance to respond as he tugged her through the garden and in the direction of Rosewood Inn.

HIGH CLASS SOCIETY SERIES

In a society of trust fund babies, millionaires and upper-class peers, four women seeking a prestigious ivy league education were thrust into a privileged world of wealth and aristocrats. Overwhelmed by the segregation they witnessed in the university that forced students to date within their own social class, they decide to create a world not based on society's rules. An organization in which the everyday woman not given the chance to date a person of caliber can overcome the barriers placed before her and date whomever she pleases.

There are no limits to finding love and they simply supply women the tools and encouragement to go after the person they want in hopes that it results in a successful relationship. Hence, after graduating from college in 2006, High Class Society Incorporated was established. Now, years later, although all four founding women have established successful careers, the secret organization is in full effect. But like every secret society, the biggest obstacle is keeping it a secret.

Blue Sapphire Temptation by Sherelle Green (Book 1)

Her Sweetest Seduction by Angela Seals (Book 2)

Sealed with a Kiss by Angela Seals (Book 3)

Passionate Persuasion by Sherelle Green (Book 4)

MEET LOGAN "LO" AND TRISTAN

Logan "Lo" Sapphire has never backed down from a challenge, so she's convinced that she can persuade the stern and unyielding self-made millionaire to keep High Class Society a secret after he bursts into her office demanding to know his sister's whereabouts. The last thing Lo wants to do is go on a wild goose chase with a walking sex ad to find his sister, but maybe, just maybe, finding her will coax him into signing a confidentiality agreement.

Tristan Derrington has a reputation for doing what he wants, when he wants. Usually nothing will stop Tristan from pursuing a gorgeous beauty like Logan, but even temptation in four-inch heels won't stand in the way of him finding his sister and exposing HCS. He may think he has a solid plan to avoid their obvious attraction, but even the best laid plans can fail. The more time they spend together, the harder it is to deny their explosive chemistry. Especially when they realize how delicious giving into temptation can be.

EXCERPT: BLUE SAPPHIRE TEMPTATION

Prologue

January 2006
Yale University

"That's it! I'm done wasting my time on these snobbish boys who think more with their wallets than their minds."

Logan Sapphire looked up from her notebook as her friend Harper Rose entered their apartment.

"I'm guessing the date didn't go well."

Harper huffed. "Let's try terrible. Horrible. Possibly the worst date of my entire life."

"Maybe you're forgetting about that frat guy you went out with two months ago," said their other roommate, Peyton Davis, as she entered the living room and took a seat on the chair opposite Logan. "If I remember correctly, he rushed your date because he had to take out that freshman and he actually had the nerve to tell you that."

"Oh right," Harper said as she kicked off her heels and plopped on the couch. "Yeah, he was pretty bad."

All three ladies glanced at the door as their fourth roommate, Savannah Westbrook, entered the apartment lugging a book bag, tote bag, and laptop bag that she immediately dropped at the entrance. Logan never did understand why Savannah always carried around so much stuff, but that was Savannah. She was always researching, studying, or doing something that required her to take her notes, books and laptop everywhere.

"What did I miss?" Savannah asked as she sat on the couch next to Harper.

Harper sighed. "Just me ranting about my sorry excuse for a date with that arrogant jerk I went out with tonight."

"Wait, isn't he that fine guy from your photo journalism class that you were dying to go out with? I thought he seemed different than the others."

"They're all the same," Harper replied. "Not only did he spend most the night talking about himself, his money, and his dad's company that he was going to be working at right after graduation. But then he had the nerve to slip me a key card for the hotel room he'd booked for the night."

"What did you tell him?" Logan asked. Harper was the insightful one in the group so there was no doubt in her mind that Harper tried to explain to him exactly why he was an arrogant jerk instead of just cursing him out. She was the one who didn't just take things from surface value, but instead, she always took a deeper look.

"He told me that most women would jump at the opportunity to have sex with him on a first date. So I told him all the reasons why he would never get into my panties."

"The nerve of these guys. See, this is the only reason why I regret not going to a regular university. There are some real pretentious assholes here," Peyton chimed in.

"And even if you're lucky enough to find a *trust fund* guy here who is actually decent, you run into issues with his friends and family accepting you," Logan added. Although she was currently engaged to one of those *privileged* men and had been dating him for most of college, she couldn't help that feeling in the pit of her stomach. That feeling that warned her she was making the wrong decision by marrying him after college and joining a family that didn't accept her or think she was worthy enough to carry their last name. She didn't date him for his money, but his family didn't see it that way.

"We aren't the only women with these issues," Savannah stated. "Just last week, I was talking to perky Paula, who couldn't stop crying in class after her boyfriend of three years broke up with her."

Logan shook her head in disbelief. "They were so in love. Please tell me it's not because her family had to file for bankruptcy."

"You guessed it," Savannah confirmed. "Apparently, being with someone who no longer has money isn't a good look. Three years down the drain."

"See, I worked my ass off to get here," Harper said. "Being from a low or middle-class family shouldn't make me less worthy of love than someone born from money. Isn't love about finding your soul mate and the person you want to spend the rest of your life with? Wouldn't you rather have a hardworking woman by your side, money or no money?"

Peyton leaned over and slapped hands with Harper. "Agreed. And the opening line on a date shouldn't be how much my family makes or how dating me can improve or decrease their social status."

Logan glanced around at her friends as they began

sharing stories that they'd heard around campus from women who had fallen for a guy only to realize that because of social status, they couldn't be together. Logan and her roommates were all from hard-working families and each had worked hard to get accepted into Yale on scholarship and follow their dreams. They didn't major in the same discipline, but they'd instantly connected during freshman orientation week and had been close all through college. Even though it was their last semester, she was certain they would remain friends after graduation and already, the four-some was planning on moving to New York together.

"You know what's crazy," Logan said finally closing her notebook and placing it on the coffee table. "We each gained so much by attending Yale, but I think you all agree that we've never faced this much adversity when it came to dating and by the sound of it, there are so many ladies on campus that are in the same boat as we are. And not just here at Yale, I'm sure this is an issue outside of school as well."

Harper nodded her head in agreement. "I think you're right. My cousin went through a similar issue with liking a man she met at a business conference. She said he was really interested in her as well, but after spending the first two conference days together, he was pulled in several different directions by other women."

"So he just stopped talking to her?" Logan asked.

"Sort of. See, at her company she's an executive assistant, which is a great position and she really loves it. She accompanied the president of her company on the trip. But the women approaching the man she was interested in were all VP's, Presidents of other companies or women who were part of a family that sponsored the conference. Since his organization was planning the conference, his job as

CEO of the event was to wine and dine all clients to try and get new business."

Logan began seeing the bigger picture. "So basically, he was interested, but because of obligations to talk to the other women, he couldn't spend as much time with her."

"That's right. But I told her that I felt like she should have just continued to talk to him like she had been. She wasn't invited to every event at the conference, but she was invited to enough where she could have pushed past those women and made an effort."

"Easier said than done," Savannah said. "It's one thing to know a man is interested. It's another issue entirely to have the confidence not to care about what the other people in attendance think and convince yourself that you're bold enough to talk to him."

"I agree with Savannah," Peyton said. "Sometimes it's about self-confidence and the idea that you aren't any different than the other women vying for his attention. All men who have money or were born from money don't only want to date women from influential families. We run into that a lot here at Yale, but I guess we have to keep in mind that we are dealing with boys trying to be men. Not men who already know what they want and don't care about what others think."

"Those men are out there," Logan added with a sly smile. "We just have to find them."

Harper squinted her eyes at Logan. "Lo, I know that look. What are you thinking?"

"Do you guys remember last year when we were sitting around drinking wine after celebrating Savannah's twenty-first birthday?"

They all nodded their head in agreement. "Do you remember what we discussed that night?"

Savannah scrunched her head in thought. "Was that the time we stayed up all night discussing what it would be like in a world that didn't have typical dating rules that you had to follow? I think we talked about how it would be if we could date good men and not worry about whether or not money, family names, or social standing would be an issue."

"Exactly," Logan said snapping her fingers. "Peyton, you said you would love it if we could start our own organization. Then Harper, you started talking about how great it would be if it were a secret organization that no one knew about. Then Savannah, you and I started talking about the way the organization could work and how great it would be if we also encouraged women to pursue love and help build their self-esteem. Especially if their self-esteem was damaged as a result of a bad relationship."

"Um, so what exactly are you getting at?" Peyton asked inquisitively. "Because it sounds a lot like you're trying to say we should turn the ideas we had that day into reality."

Logan smiled and clasped her hands together as she looked at each roommate.

"Oh no," Savannah said shaking her head. "That's precisely what you're trying to say isn't it?"

"Come on guys, you all have to admit that our ideas that night were pretty amazing."

"I'm pretty sure I was tipsy," Harper mentioned.

"No you weren't. We had just started drinking our first glass when we talked about this." Logan got up from her chair and began pacing the room as her brain began working overtime.

"Hear me out ladies. Peyton, you have amazing business sense and there is no doubt in my mind that you have what it takes to handle the ins and outs of a secret organization. Savannah, you're amazing at researching and like we discussed last year, it would be great if we could develop profiles of eligible bachelors, but they have to be the right type of men. Harper, you're a wiz with marketing and social media. Private or not, we will definitely need that. And of course, since I'm majoring in human resources, I could handle meeting and conversing with the members."

She turned and was greeted with blank stares from all three women, so she continued talking. "I know we would have to work out a lot of kinks and really solidify our business plan, but there is no doubt in my mind that we were on to something great the night of Savannah's birthday and I'm sure, if we put our minds to it, we could create something amazing. A secret society unlike any other."

When their faces still displayed blank stares, she'd thought maybe she was talking too fast and they hadn't heard her. She was relieved when Harper's mouth curled to the side in a smile.

"I can't believe I'm saying this, but I honestly loved the idea when we first came up with it last year, and I love it even more now that we're graduating. Off hand, I can already think about several women who would be more than happy to join."

"So, we're really going to do this?" Savannah said with a smile. "We are actually going to start our own secret society?"

"Not just any society," Peyton said as she stood to join Logan. "Didn't we create some guidelines for the organization that night?"

"I think I have all our notes from that," Logan said as she ran to her room to grab her laptop and returned to the living room. She kneeled down at the coffee table, opened up a word document, and was joined by Harper, Savannah and Peyton who kneeled down around her laptop as well.

"Here it is. All our notes from that night."

Savannah pointed to sentence. "Oh wow, it says here that we thought members should have to take a rigorous personal, professional and spiritual assessment when they join before they are placed in a position to meet quality matches."

Harper pointed to another sentence. "And here it says that we will build well-researched profiles on eligible bachelors and give women the tools and encouragement to go after the man of their dreams."

"So we decided that this wouldn't be a match making service right?" Peyton asked the group. "We would place women in a position to meet a man they are interested in, but we aren't playing matchmaker and setting them up on a date."

"That seems accurate to what we discussed," Logan answered. "But of course, we'll have to get all those details nailed down before inviting members."

"Didn't we come up with a name too?" Peyton asked searching the notes on the page.

Logan scrolled down until she landed on the page she was searching for.

"High Class Society Incorporated," she said aloud to the group. "That was the name we created last year."

Harper clasped her hands together. "Oh I remember now! I still love that name."

"Me too," Savannah and Peyton said in unison.

Logan pointed her finger to the words on the screen written underneath the name of the organization and read them aloud. "There are no limits to finding love, no rulebook to discover your soul mate, and no concrete path to follow in order to reach your destiny. In High Class Society, we make that journey a little easier. High Class Society ... where elite and ordinary meet."

She looked up at each of the ladies, each with a knowing gleam in their eyes. This year didn't just mark their graduation and start of their careers. It also marked the beginning of a new chapter for the four of them. A chapter that was sure to be filled with pages and pages of new self-discoveries

Chapter 1

9 years later...

"You have *one* minute to tell me where the hell my sister is, or I'll have no choice but to call the authorities and expose this disgraceful ass company."

The deep timbre in the man's voice bounced off the burgundy walls of the Manhattan office and teased Logan's ears. Her big, doe-eyes stared at the sexy intruder with the rich, mocha skin tone as she tried her best not to drop her mouth open in admiration. She knew who he was. Her company had done their research on him when Logan had first met his sister. They were actually in the process of gathering further information on him to build a more solid profile and add him to their list of exceptional men. However, the pictures definitely didn't do this former Canadian turned New Yorker justice.

In the profile she'd received from her partner and friend, Savannah Westbrook, the Director of Research and Development for High Class Society, she could tell he was a walking sex ad. Even after recognizing his clearly masculine sex appeal, she couldn't have prepared herself for the onslaught of pleasure she'd feel coming face-to-face with temptation.

Her eyes wandered up and down the length of his body that was encased in a deep-blue Tom Ford suit, complementing leather shoes, and a classic navy-blue watch with gold trimmings. Licking her lips as she admired his six-foot frame, she tried not to imagine how enticing he'd look without a stitch of clothing on. Usually Logan was attracted to men with curly hair and a caramel complexion, but the man standing before her didn't have either of those qualities … and damned if she even cared. Within a few seconds, she'd dismissed every physical characteristic she'd ever believed she wanted in a man. *Delicious,* she thought after taking note of his short fade and chiseled jawline, his neatly groomed features mirroring that of a Tyson Beckford look-alike rather than Shemar Moore.

"I'm so sorry, Lo," said her assistant, Nina, a grad student at Columbia University, as she came rushing in to the office behind the unwelcomed guest. "I'm not sure how he even got clearance into the building or how he found your office."

"It wasn't hard to find your office with so few people here and a distracted security guard," he explained, his eyes never straying from Logan. His piercing gaze was so intense that Logan was glad she was sitting at her desk or she would have surely faltered. "And you should really lock up the bathroom window in the basement. I climbed right in."

She tilted her head to the side, unable to believe that a man of his status would climb through a window to get into their office.

"It's okay, Nina," she reassured, refusing to break their stare-down. "I'll listen to what Mr. Derrington has to say."

Nina hesitantly exited the office and left the door cracked, instead of closing it all the way like she normally would when Logan had a meeting.

"Ms. Sapphire, I take it that you already know who I am," he stated with a slight curl of his lips. *Don't do that,* she thought when he walked a little closer to her desk. His imposing stance was already sending her body into a frenzy. She couldn't stay seated and let him have the upper hand.

"It appears you already know who I am as well, Mr. Derrington." Rising from her seat, she noted the appreciative glance he shot in her direction. She smoothed out her designer skirt and blouse before sitting on the edge of her desk. His eyes ventured to her creamy, maple thighs before making their way to the swell of her breasts.

Logan's breath caught as she watched him observe her. She was hardly showing any cleavage and her clothes were concealing all of her assets. Yet the way he was staring at her, made her feel as if she wasn't wearing anything at all. The air around them was thick with awareness, and the silence almost caused her to fidget under his stare.

"I've been away on business and came back early because I hadn't heard from my younger sister. So I went to her condo, and imagine my surprise when I surfed her laptop, trying to find some information about her whereabouts, and saw several screen shots saved in a folder on her desktop entitled High Class Society Incorporated."

Logan winced at his statement, silently cursing his discovery. HCS prided themselves on being paperless, a key to keeping the organization a secret. Unfortunately, no matter how good their small IT team was, some things were hard to avoid ... like members taking screen shots containing information that couldn't get out to the public.

"Ms. Sapphire, after I got over the shock of an organization like yours existing, I researched the duties of the founders listed on one of the screen shots and realized that you may be the only person to know where my sister is.

According to what I read, all women are supposed to check in daily with you if they're away with a prospect, correct?"

"That is true," Logan responded. "May I remind you that the contents on those screen shots are private, and my organization did not approve for your sister to go off on her own before finishing part two of her orientation session, including our policy on safety."

"So she *is* with a man," he said more to himself than her. His jaw twitched and he placed both hands in his pockets, frustration radiating from his body. "May I remind *you* that as long as my sister is missing, everything is my business. She wouldn't have gotten this idea to run off with God knows who if your company didn't exist."

"We help women find the person of their dreams, Mr. Derrington. We have rules, which she didn't follow. We aren't babysitters."

"I assume I don't need to reinforce that I'll sue you for all your worth if you don't tell me what I need to know, Ms. Sapphire ... if that's even your real last name."

"It is," she stated firmly. "I have nothing to hide, and although this is against my better judgment, I will tell you who she's with," she continued, purposely leaving out the fact that she didn't know where Sophia was. She did have something to hide, but she needed to bluff to buy her and her partners some time before he went to the authorities.

"So," he said, removing both hands from his pockets and waving them for her to explain, "who is my sister with?"

Logan sighed, still not okay with sharing the information, but she knew he wasn't leaving without an answer. "She's with social media prodigy, Justice Covington."

She watched all of the color drain from his face while both hands curled into fists. His breathing grew heavier and he slowly rolled his neck ... purposeful ... measured. Logan found her own breathing growing labored as she sat and watched a range of emotions cross his face.

"Then we definitely have a problem," he stated as he released his fists and leaned in closer to her, "because Justice Covington met my sister when she was eighteen and they tried to get married two years ago. If we don't find them, he may finally get his wish ... *if* they haven't tied the knot already."

***

30 minutes earlier ...

"Where are you?" Logan Sapphire asked aloud as she scrolled through the online files she had for one of the newest clients to High Class Society, Sophia Derrington. Her cherry-colored office desk—that was usually extremely organized—was covered in an array of paperwork and maps she'd printed to try and piece together where Sophia might be. In all of her eight years of being Director of HR and Recruiting, she'd never lost contact with a client for this long.

"What the hell am I going to do?" she huffed aloud, standing up and running her French tipped fingernails through her thick and wavy copper-colored hair. She paced back and forth in her office, glad that her partners had all retired for the night. Only Logan and her assistant remained, and she was extremely thankful that Nina had decided to help her search for Sophia, despite the fact that Nina felt partially responsible.

Sophia hadn't been born from wealth, but thirty-four-year-old Tristan Derrington, Sophia's older brother, was a self-made millionaire and one of the most sought after custom watch designers in the country. He created top-notch designs for numerous celebrities, singers, hip-hop artists, and political figures. High Class Society had certain rules, and one of them was to ensure that the only women allowed in the society were women who weren't born from money or from highly privileged families. They were all successful professionals and entrepreneurs, or self-made millionaires. Of course, sometimes rules were meant to be broken, and in some instances, they made an exception and allowed a woman to join who was born from money or a well-known family. Those situations were handled on a case-by-case basis.

Even though it seemed unfair, Logan and her partners had strict rules that they had to adhere to in order to ensure that High Class Society was successful and effective. They didn't just let any woman into the organization. Each woman went through a psychological, spiritual, and professional screening to ensure that they were truly looking for love and not a gold-digging groupie. Their clientele consisted of women of different nationalities, ethnic backgrounds, and occupations, and they were proud of the successful relationships that had developed from their company.

Logan stopped pacing and abruptly sat down in her desk chair, accidently knocking over a cup of black coffee as she did so. "Shit," she cursed, quickly grabbing some nearby napkins and dabbing up the coffee.

"Are you okay?" Nina yelled from outside of her office.

"I'm fine," she yelled back after she'd wiped up most of the coffee and waved the wet stained paperwork in the air to dry it quicker.

Focus, Logan! she thought to herself as she leaned back

in her chair and clasped her hands in her lap. *Are there any clues in the last conversation you had with Sophia?*

Ever since she'd first met Sophia months ago, the twenty-four year old had wormed her way into Logan's heart after divulging the story about how she'd lost the only man she had ever loved and was ready to see what else was out there. She'd claimed she needed High Class Society, and Logan had chosen to ignore the signs that something more was going on. Now that she had no idea where Sophia had run off to, she had time to reflect on the fact that Sophia had only shown interest in one man ... Justice Covington. HCS always listed possible matches in each woman's personal online folder and Sophia had included other men in her profile as "persons of interest," but any time Logan had spoken with Sophia, the young lady had only asked her about Justice, the thirty-two-year-old brain behind an up and coming social media network.

Closing her eyes, she thought back to the information she'd given Sophia about Justice attending a Broadway play at the Ethel Barrymore Theatre here in New York. She had warned Sophia to focus on men closer to her own age, but she'd been determined to meet Justice. That was the last day they'd spoken almost two weeks ago. Since then, she'd only received one text from Sophia saying that she was okay and was following her heart. All of their HCS ladies knew they had to check in daily if they were going away with a man, so she was worried and pissed that Sophia was jeopardizing the company and going rogue.

"What am I missing?" she wondered aloud before going on her computer to look at the personal file they had on Justice Covington again. There was a reason Sophia was interested in Justice, and why Savannah hadn't been able to track Justice's whereabouts lately in regards to his relation-ship status. Something wasn't adding up.

"Sir, you can't go in there," she heard Nina yell right before a man walked into her office, literally taking her breath away. *Tristan Derrington ... in the flesh.* God, he was sexy. Although she wished she could relish in his presence, the fact that he was standing in her office meant that HCS was in more trouble than she knew.

ABOUT THE AUTHOR

Sherelle Green is a Chicago native with a dynamic imagination and a passion for reading and writing. Ever since she was a little girl, Sherelle has enjoyed story-telling. Upon receiving her BA in English, she decided to test her skills by composing a fifty-page romance. The short, but sweet, story only teased her creative mind, but it gave her the motivation she needed to follow her dream of becoming a published author.

Sherelle loves connecting with readers and other literary enthusiasts, and she is a member of RWA and NINC. She's also an Emma award winner and two-time RT Book Reviews nominee. Sherelle enjoys composing novels that are emotionally driven and convey real relationships and real-life issues that touch on subjects that may pull at your heartstrings. Nothing satisfies her more than writing stories filled with compelling love affairs, multifaceted char-acters, and intriguing relationships.

For more information:
www.sherellegreen.com
authorsherellegreen.com

ALSO BY SHERELLE GREEN

An Elite Event Series:
A Tempting Proposal
If Only for Tonight
Red Velvet Kisses
Beautiful Surrender

Bare Sophistication Series:
Enticing Winter
Falling for Autumn
Waiting for Summer
Nights of Fantasy
Her Unexpected Valentine

High Class Society Series:
Blue Sapphire Temptation
Passionate Persuasion

Additional Books:
A Los Angeles Passion
A Miami Affair
Wrapped in Red